POLYBIUS
THE URBAN LEGEND

ANDY BRIGGS

IT'S NOT JUST A GAME...

INTRODUCTION

Spy Quest is more than just a book - it's an entire immersive adventure game that you can play at:

www.spy-quest.com

Uniquely it is also available for you to play in hotels and resorts around the world - from the UK to the USA and Mexico! So you have no excuse to be bored on holiday - you can be a **real** member of the Spy Quest Agency!

Check out the list at the back of the book, for where you can play it and follow us @SpyQuest for the latest news about upcoming books!

Download the free Spy Quest app from iTunes and select 'Spy Cam', then hold the camera over the illustrations to discover the secrets hidden within the book.

Now, turn the page... and let the adventure begin!

IT'S NOT JUST A GAME...

Published in 2015 by Polybius Publishing
an imprint of Polybius Games Ltd
31 Clarkin Avenue, East Kilbride, G75 9GS
United Kingdom
www.polybiuspublishing.com

ISBN: 978-0-9932831-0-9

Printed and bound in Great Britain by Clays Ltd, St Ives plc

CONTENTS

Chapter 1 - THE PAST *7*

Chapter 2 - GAMING FOR GEEKS *17*

Chapter 3 - GLENDEVON CASTLE HOTEL *29*

Chapter 4 - UNEXPECTED EVENTS *45*

Chapter 5 - THE WRONG RECRUIT *59*

Chapter 6 - THE CHASE IS ON *73*

Chapter 7 - PARIS *93*

Chapter 8 - TRACKING THE ENEMY *119*

Chapter 9 - CAPTIVE *137*

Chapter 10 - THE LYCORTAS EFFECT *151*

Chapter 11 - THE ESCAPE *165*

CONTENTS

CHAPTER ONE

THE PAST

Kevin bowed his head against the driving rain. As far as he could remember it had rained every day since he had been in England so he should be used to it by now, but he wasn't at all. He hated it as much as he hated the fact he had been forced to move here with his parents, far from the sunny shores of California.

He was now convinced that rain was the usual weather for this sleepy seaside town. He hurried towards his destination, drawn to the colourful neon lights like a moth to a lamp.

It was a bright and busy computer arcade. Kevin grinned as he looked around the welcoming sight. Dozens of tall wooden cabinets housed state-of-the art computer games. Children of every age clustered around them, cheering the players on, pressing greasy fingers against the screens, while the players guided characters with knobbly joysticks and colourful buttons. The heady mix of electronic music, beeps and chirps of the games filled his ears. The arcade's exciting atmosphere always made Kevin grin no matter how bad his day had been. He was glad he was alive now, in the 1980s, to witness what he assumed must be the height of computer technology. How could it possibly get any better?

His usual favourites, Pac-man and Asteroids, were surrounded by older kids who looked in no rush to leave. Kevin searched for a free machine, one hand jingling the pocket money in his pocket that his Gran had given him. It seemed that every machine was taken. He knew he should have arrived earlier, but his mother had forced him to finish his dinner before he was allowed out.

He pushed his way past the crowds gathered around the change booth where Mrs Carroll was constantly breaking down one-pound notes into ten pence coins for the gamers. Kevin spotted Mr Carroll in the far corner of the arcade, amongst the less popular gambling games. He was crouching behind a new machine, stretching to plug it into the socket although his meaty arms barely fitted through the gap between the cabinet and the wall.

"Evening, Mr. Carroll!" chirped Kevin.

Mr Carroll flinched - banging his head against the machine's overhanging console as he turned to look at Kevin.

"OW! Blimey, Kevin! You ought to stop creeping up on folks like that! Nearly gave me a heart attack!"

A cigarette wobbled from Mr Carroll's lips, and Kevin resisted pointing out that they were more likely to give him a heart attack. Instead, Kevin examined the new machine. It was a tall black wooden cabinet with plastic green and red stripes providing the only colour. It was drab compared to the other games. Kevin didn't recognise the logo - a single eye in a circle that was made out of tiny numbers: zeroes and ones. He recognised it as binary, the language of computers.

"Is this a new game?" asked Kevin. He expected it to be another dull poker machine since Mr Carroll was setting it up in the gambling section.

"Aye, it is. Odd thing too. We weren't expecting

a delivery this month, but it turned up in a crate outside the door. In the pouring rain mark you. That's why I set it over here. No room for it."

With a grunt, Mr Carroll plugged the machine in, and then rolled it back against the wall. They looked at the screen expectantly. Lines of code ran across it; white text against black. As Kevin watched he was suddenly aware that the name of the game was not written anywhere. Where the lettering should have been was just the binary eye. The longer he stared at the eye, the more piercing the gaze appeared to be...

The machine bleeped and the screen flashed once, jolting him from his daydream. Another flash... then the screen remained blank. After several painful seconds, a word appeared.

"Polybius," read Kevin and rested one hand on the stumpy joystick, and the other on the two coloured fire controls: one red, the other white. Then another message blinked up: INSERT 10p.

Kevin glanced at Mr Carroll, but knew better than to ask for a free go. Mr Carroll and his wife owned the arcade and were always friendly to the local kids, but they drew the line at charity.

Kevin pulled a fist full of coins from his pocket. A few pennies, more two and five pence pieces as well as the annoying half penny coins. Amongst them were five gleaming ten pence coins. Mr Carroll saw the money and nodded approvingly.

"Let me know what you think of it," he said, patting the machine before heading off to help his wife in the change booth.

Based on the bland case design, Kevin didn't have high expectations for the game he was about to play. He shoved the ten pence into the slot and heard it clatter into the empty metal cash box locked away in the heart of the machine. At least he would be the first ever to play this game in his town, maybe even the whole country. The world even!

As he rested his hands on the controls he felt the familiar thrill he always experienced after he'd spent forty minutes loading up a game at home on his brand new Commodore Vic 20 computer. It had been a present from his parents when they had moved. The games helped ease the pain of leaving his friends behind and made him feel privileged, as hardly any of his friends had a computer at home.

The Polybius screen flashed and vector graphics crisscrossed in a whirl of colours. The lines formed a tunnel and he was immediately speeding along shooting odd shaped villains that zoomed towards him. His fingers rhythmically tapped the buttons and his onscreen character fired lasers and missiles that detonated the bad guys in a shower of pixels.

Kevin was instantly addicted. The controls were straightforward and he had managed to get into the game without reading through any instructions. Branching tunnels appeared - not just left and right but also up and down. Unusual pairs of symbols marked each branch. Every time Kevin took a branching tunnel the screen would flicker and his head would hurt as if a headache had just jumped into his forehead, beaten up his brain, then jumped out again.

After a minute, Kevin started to think that the symbols had some meaning, a hidden code. He wasn't aware what it was, or even how he had come to that conclusion, but the fact he hadn't been killed yet meant he was doing something right.

The screen continued to flash with more regularity. Kevin was sure he saw numbers and letters in those brief whiteouts, and when the flashes faded they left an afterimage on the back of his eye - which seemed to overlay with the action on the screen and revealed an even more complex series of equations he couldn't decipher. But it was all over in seconds and Kevin's attention was drawn back to the game that was becoming increasingly fast and furious.

From across the arcade, Mr Carroll changed a pair of pound notes for some spotty teenagers, before glancing across at Kevin. The boy was still frantically hammering the buttons so Mr Carroll assumed the game was addictive, which was good news. The bad news was that he hadn't seen Kevin put in any more than his original ten pence. Mr Carroll didn't want games that were too easy or else he'd never make any money.

The clatter of three fifty pence coins drew his attention back to the counter. Mr Carroll changed them to smaller denominations for a boy who was eager to resume his game as the INSERT COINS TO CONTINUE countdown spiralled towards zero. The ten-pees were snatched before they hit the counter and the boy ran back to the game.

Mr Carroll glanced back at Kevin.

He was gone.

With a frown, Mr Carroll looked around. There was only one way in and out of the arcade and the boy had been hooked on the game only seconds before and had plenty of coinage to pay for several more games. The Polybius machine was dark once more, with only the simple logo on the screen. Mr Carroll's attention was drawn back to the counter as another group of teenagers demanded change.

He was the last person to see Kevin. Even after a nationwide missing person campaign.

Even stranger, when Mr Carroll opened the arcade the following day to show the police the game Kevin had been playing - the machine was gone.

It had vanished without a trace.

Polybius...the arcade machine

CHAPTER TWO

GAMING FOR GEEKS

Total concentration. That's what Sam Rayner needed to complete his mission. Complete and utter devotion to the task in hand. He focused, fearing to blink in case he missed his target. He tried to blot out every sensation, every sound.

"Sam!" came the faint irritating voice.

Sam's eyes narrowed. His sweaty palms nearly dropped his weapon of choice.

"Sam!" repeated the voice, this time it was louder.

"We're moving into position," crackled another boy's voice over his headset.

"Roger!" acknowledged Sam. The rest of his team were in action, relying on him to do his task. Teamwork was the only way they could possibly hope to win the war.

Then he saw his target - a large tank, barely visible through the rubble and burnt trees at the end of the street. He would have to get closer, and that meant the possibility of alerting the enemy troops hidden around him. He had no choice.

"I see it, but I'm too far away for a clear shot. Got to get closer."

"OK," said the voice over his headset. "Be careful."

Sam edged from cover. A quick look around the street didn't reveal any enemy activity so he took his chance. He made it halfway down the street before something struck him hard on the arm - forcing him to run into a crumbling wall.

"SAM!" screamed the irritating voice in his ear.

Sam looked around to see his sister's face was centimetres from his. It was creased in a scowl. Sam was growing more convinced that the scowl was Rebecca's natural expression.

"I've been calling you!" she shouted, despite the fact she had torn his headset off.

Sam groped to retrieve it, but Rebecca held it

just out of reach. He could already hear the sound of gunfire and his companions yelling.

"Give me that back! We're in the middle of an operation!" he hissed. He looked back to his target in time to see an explosion close by, followed by half a dozen enemy soldiers appearing around the corner and raising their weapons at him.

"NO!" yelled Sam - but it was too late. Multiple shots struck his virtual soldier who collapsed to the floor, oozing digital blood.

"Well you're dead now," said Rebecca calmly - then she snatched the remote control and turned the television off.

"What have you done?" squeaked Sam. He was trying not to shout, but it was difficult to control his temper under such provocation. "It took us ages to get to that level! We were almost at the end of the game!"

"It's only a stupid game," sniffed Rebecca. "Anyway, dinner's ready. Mum has been shouting you forever."

"That could have waited," said Sam who had lived on reheated meals all autumn half-term. "This was important!"

Rebecca shook her head. "When will you grow up?"

"Grow up? I'm twelve!"

"Duh! We're twins. I know that! I mean grow out of playing silly computer games."

Sam threw his controller down and followed his sister into the kitchen. In the good old days he would have retaliated with a punch to the arm for what she had done, but the endless trouble that placed him in had eventually convinced him that it wasn't worth it. Besides, there were smarter ways of getting revenge.

When Rebecca had pleaded to their parents for a mobile phone, Sam had stolen it one night and swapped all the phone numbers around so Rebecca had never been sure who she had really been texting when she was gossiping about her friends. Sam was delighted to see that ruse didn't win her any popularity contests in school. Another time, while shopping, he had attached a security tag from a clothes shop to her coat so she set off the alarms in almost every store they visited. Each time Sam took revenge he knew Rebecca couldn't prove he had done anything, even if she suspected so. That made it even sweeter.

Sam slouched at the table where his mother and father were already eating, their gaze fixed to a gloomy soap opera playing on the television positioned at the end of the counter. His mum glanced at him and flashed a smile.

"You're finally here! Help yourself. It's your favourite, my world famous spaghetti." Then she turned back to the television.

Sam scooped a forkful of sludgy pasta. He decoded what his mum had said: "favourite" she meant the one he hated the most, and "world famous" she meant because people across the globe avoided it at all costs. The spaghetti was so congealed that the fork stood up on its own inside the bowl.

"Playing secret agent again?" said dad without taking his eyes off the TV.

"Yes, and I'd nearly completed the level on multiplayer mode before the nerdinator here ruined the whole thing!"

Rebecca scowled at her brother. She hated the nickname Sam had created, it was just because she studied hard to get good marks in school. What annoyed her was the fact Sam never studied but always did equally as well. It was because of his good grades that his parents allowed him to play so many computer games without interfering.

"That's nice," said mum without taking her eyes from the soap opera.

Sam played with his food, chopping it into ever-smaller pieces. It beat actually eating it.

"Another five minutes and I could have won that million pound prize," said Sam. Rebecca shot him another evil look. His parents stared at the television.

"Well done, son," said dad on autopilot.

Sam sighed and put his fork down. "Finished." He glared at Rebecca, silently daring her to snitch on him. For a change she remained quiet and brushed her long brown hair behind her ear, clipping it in place with one of hundreds of long metal hair grips she kept on her person at all times. Sam dumped the contents of his plate in the bin, placed the plate in the dishwasher and took three pieces of fruit before heading back to his game.

It was a pointless endeavour. His virtual team had long since been defeated and had gone offline. Sam didn't have the heart to start the game all over again with a new team. Instead, he picked up a book - a new spy thriller. It was part of a series he was rapidly becoming addicted to. He'd enjoyed them so much that he had begun to neglect his hobby, dabbling as an amateur magician. He'd learnt most of the tricks from the Internet and had just perfected picking handcuff locks for an escapism routine before his father had given him the novel.

The story was a welcome break from the game. He loved games but no matter how impressive the graphics and gameplay were, he knew they were just fake simulations compared to his own vivid imagination. He often dreamt about how terrific it would be to be a spy in exotic countries, experiencing real danger; but he realised that it was an unlikely goal. He had once surfed the Internet, scouring through job sites to see if any of them advertised "spy" as a job. After several months of fruitless searching he had given up and decided to focus on a more realistic goal.

Many of his friends wanted to be professional footballers when they left school, but Sam wanted to be a professional games player. His sister had predictably laughed when he announced his new career plan. Even when he showed her that teams around the world earned thousands by playing games against each other. In Korea it was even a national spectator sport worth millions! However, now he was starting to wonder if even that was a realistic job. Being old must be boring!

With a deep sigh he took the novel and headed for the peace and solitude of his bedroom.

When Sam woke up the next morning, he had no idea how the day's events were set to lead him on an extraordinary and dangerous adventure.

It started as usual. His blissful lie-in was shattered by his sister shouting about losing something or other. A pillow across his ears failed to blot out the nasal shrieking. To make matters worse, his parents insisted they all go shopping together so they could plan the week's meals. Apparently Sam's pasta sabotage hadn't gone unnoticed and his mum now insisted he needed to be there to pick his own meals if he didn't want to starve to death.

Cruising down the endless supermarket aisles was mind-numbingly boring. Sam made the most of the situation by taking along his handheld games console and playing a new first-person shooter his dad had bought him the previous week, entitled CODE ONE. It wasn't a bad game as it incorporated some difficult problem solving with shooting bad guys.

Sam had raced through the levels but had eventually been troubled by a logical problem that involved opening a door by turning various tumblers that were spread across a room. The problem was that when one tumbler was turned it would turn another one half way across the room - usually that would be the tumbler Sam had only just set. Sam knew that it was just a matter of logically working out how the tumblers were connected, but it was so frustrating that he had stopped playing the game for the last few days.

However, now he was standing opposite the baked beans, the solution suddenly revealed itself. Sam's fingers darted across the control pad and he felt a thrill of excitement as the tumblers finally rotated into the correct position and the door opened in a blaze of light. He hurried his character through the portal and was surprised to see the words:

GAME OVER

"Huh?" he blurted aloud. It had been a good

game, but rather short. He was about to complain but another message appeared:

CONGRATULATIONS! YOU HAVE QUALIFIED FOR THE PRO-GAMER LITE CHAMPIONSHIP!

Sam's mouth went dry. The PGLC, was the biggest gathering of game players in the country. It was the video game equivalent of junior league footballers being talent spotted by the bigger clubs.

This was how people became professional gamers!

The message faded from the screen. Sam panicked. He hadn't had any time to enter his details, how would they know who he was? He pressed every button, but the elusive message refused to appear onscreen again.

He spent the rest of the shopping trip sulking in silence. By the time he returned home, Sam had convinced himself that it was just a joke that everybody saw at the end of the level.

As they entered the house a single message greeted them on the answering machine. Everybody's hands were full carrying the shopping, so it was ten minutes later, after everything had been stored away, before Sam's dad played the message back.

"This is a message for Sam Rayner. Congratulations, Sam, you have won a place at the PGLC tournament this Monday. You and your family are cordially invited to come to the Glendevon Castle Hotel in Scotland..."

Sam was so excited that the rest of the message passed in a haze. There was a phone number for Sam's dad to call back. It took several attempts to convince his parents that it was a serious offer before his dad finally dialled the number and had a hushed conversation with the person on the other end of the line.

When he hung up, his smile betrayed the good news.

"Sam's only gone and won us a holiday at a luxury hotel! Pack your bags!"

For Sam, the very best moment was the stunned look on his sister's face. She finally found her voice, albeit with a begrudging tone.

"Well done, I s'pose. Looks like you didn't waste all your time playing those stupid games."

CHAPTER THREE
GLENDEVON CASTLE HOTEL

The trip up to Scotland was long and uneventful. Rebecca had decided not to argue with Sam because she was getting a free holiday. Sam's thoughts were swimming with notions of being selected for the professional league. Even his parents, who normally never paid too much attention to his dreams of wealth through game playing, were now encouraging him.

Sam spent most of the car journey glued to his handheld console playing Code One. Having completed it once already, he made swift progress through the levels and finished it in a record time but there was no congratulatory message when the game ended.

With only two stops, one for the toilet and

another for food and fuel, the Rayners eventually made it to Scotland. They passed through Glasgow before seeing signs for the town nearest to the country hotel destination. Sam started to get excited when his mother pointed out the brown tourist sign pointing towards 'hotels'. The GPS confirmed the next left would take them to their destination. It wasn't long before the gold lettered sign of Glendevon welcomed them.

As they drove up the driveway Sam's mum and Rebecca both let out gasps as the hotel hove into view.

"It looks like a palace!" exclaimed Rebecca.

And it did. It was like no other hotel Sam had ever seen. He knew the five star luxury resort was famous for its golf courses and the fact celebrities and even World Leaders stayed there, but even so it was still a grand looking building.

The car park was full of modest cars, not the luxury ones Sam thought people would drive if they could afford to stay here. They were filled with families who ushered their young sons and daughters inside. A banner strung across the entrance read:

WELCOME GAMERS!

Sam studied the kids entering the hotel. It

only took him one glance at their trainers, un-tucked t-shirts and occasional baseball caps to know they were all fellow competition winners.

"You should feel right at home here," said Rebecca as they pulled up.

"Yeah, it looks brilliant," said Sam admiring the building.

"I meant the fact it's full of geeks!"

Sam rolled his eyes and turned his attention back to the families entering the hotel. He prided himself on being observant and, even before his father had found a parking space, Sam had identified his main rival.

A dark skinned boy was analysing the others, tapping his hand rhythmically against his leg as he listened to a song on his MP3 player. Sam smiled to himself, from the beat of the boy's hand he could tell it was a fast paced track - the boy didn't look like the type to be into dance music, so he guessed it must be a rock song. He walked with a slightly cocky step that oozed self-confidence, and even Sam felt himself start to doubt he could beat him.

Sam shook his head; that was a stupid thought.

As far as he knew, the boy could be the worst player here. Looks can be deceiving, he reminded himself. He'd read that in his spy novel.

Sam climbed out of the car and stretched. Out of the corner of his eye he noticed a man staring at him. He was tall with dark hair and wore a long black coat, his eyes were hidden behind sunglasses, but Sam could feel the man's gaze. As soon as Sam looked straight at him the stranger took a step backwards. Groups of new arrivals cut between them and by the time they had entered the hotel the man had disappeared.

Odd...

Sam flinched when his dad suddenly gripped his shoulder. "Come on, son, let's get checked in." Sam took his backpack as his dad hauled a pair of suitcases from the car boot. "Blimey, what have you packed? We're only here for four days!" Both suitcases were big enough for a fortnight at least.

His mum and Rebecca exchanged silent glances and shook their heads, before they excitedly led the way inside.

The lobby was marble with a pair of pillars either side of the reception desk. Antiques were tastefully positioned on tables and mantles, including an old radio and a brass measuring instrument, whose purpose Sam couldn't guess at. Before they could get near, a bearded man in a kilt intercepted Sam.

"Ah, hullo! You're one of the computer kids?" Sam nodded. "Then you'll be wanting to sign up over there." He gestured towards a desk where a very efficient young woman was quickly dealing with the other families. She was Hispanic and dressed in a smart grey suit with her long black hair tied in a ponytail. She was pretty but didn't offer a smile when Sam approached.

"Name?"

"Um... Sam Rayner. We were told we'd won—"

The woman's fingers flew over a tablet computer on the desk. Sam saw his name. He cocked his head to see what else was written, but the girl angled it away so he couldn't see.

"Look into this." She pointed to a web camera. Sam turned to look at it and was about to say something before the woman continued. "Good. Put your hand here." She pointed to a flat pad that had an odd green gel across the surface. Sam placed his hand on it. After a second he heard a beep. "Good,' said the woman monotonously. She handed Sam an envelope. "Here's your suite key cards for you and your family. There is a schedule inside." She looked back at her screen with such purpose that it was clear the one-sided conversation was over.

Sam handed the envelope to his dad who just smiled bemusedly. "You can't fault her efficiency."

Sam's jaw hinged open when he saw the size of the room he had been given. Room, was an understatement – it was an entire suite with two huge beds, an en suite bathroom, and a living area with a massive television. Two long couches lay either side of a coffee table and there was a solid mahogany writing desk against one wall, with a comfortable chair drawn underneath.

An impressive set of French windows opened up to a balcony that offered a view across a lake and the golf courses beyond. His parents had the suite next door. The only major problem he could see was that he had to share this room with his sister.

Sam leapt on the bed closest to the window and immediately emptied his backpack to mark his territory. Rebecca was more interested in the view.

"This is wonderful," she remarked.

"Still think playing games is stupid?" said Sam as he checked his emails on his smartphone. He scrolled through a dozen games he'd downloaded before he found his emails.

Rebecca mumbled incoherently. She was never one to admit her mistakes and Sam intended on rubbing it in as much as possible; for the rest of her life if necessary. He had no new messages from his friends so put his phone away; no doubt they were all envious that he had qualified for the PGLC. Sam snatched a glossy card that stood on the bedside table. It looked more like a food menu, but listed a range of services the hotel provided.

"There's a heated swimming pool. You can go horse riding and play golf. There's a spa too. You and mum can do that while I'm out working on those computer games."

Rebecca didn't take the bait. Instead she took

out Sam's schedule from the envelope he had been given and browsed through it.

"Looks like you're going to be busy. In fact," she glanced at her watch, "You should be in downstairs now for the induction. You're late!"

"What?" Sam bounced off the bed and sprinted out of the room. He didn't want to be late on his first day!

Sam was late. He was out of breath too. He had asked the kilted man in reception for directions but the man's accent was so strong he hadn't understood the response. After wasting another few minutes he finally located the correct room. It was a large hall filled with computers that were arranged in threes, with the backs of the monitors facing one another in a triangle so players couldn't see what their opponents were doing. A group of people Sam's age sat in front of a stage. He'd seen most of them as he'd entered, and without parents adding to the numbers he could see it was a much smaller group than he'd first assumed. There were fourteen other combatants who all stared curiously at him as he entered the room. All but two of them were boys. Sam smiled in what he hoped was a cool way, but felt his cheeks burn as he became the centre of attention. He silently shuffled his way to the only free seat at the end of a row. It was next to the boy he had identified as his main rival.

Sam sheepishly sat down and nodded at the boy, who simply regarded him without the flicker of a smile. In fact Sam wondered if the boy was judging him on first appearances, exactly as he had done less than forty minutes ago.

"Now you are all, finally, here we can begin," boomed a voice from the stage.

Sam hadn't noticed anybody standing at the podium before, but a man, with salt-and-pepper hair and a perfectly groomed beard that clung to his chin, now stood there dressed in an impeccable grey suit. He gripped either side of the podium as his keen eyes scanned the crowd.

"My name is Dr Patrick Thorsten, but call me Dr Patrick. I oversee the Pro-Gaming Lite Championship, and you are all winners!"

Sam looked around the hall, the compliment made everybody grin.

Patrick continued. "But only one of you will leave here as a champion and the chance to join the country's largest professional gaming team where you will tour the world and earn thousands in prize money. It really is a life of luxury... and it could be yours. But it is not going to be an easy task. You will be playing in competition against one another and our leader board will show just who is the best amongst you."

A large screen behind Patrick suddenly illuminated. A slick animation danced across the screen, revealing each competitor's name. Sam was disheartened to see his name near the bottom quarter, even if it was because the list was in alphabetical order.

"It is very simple, you get a point for a win and nothing if you lose. We will be playing a variety of combat, strategy and racing games. They will test every aspect of your abilities. Plus, be on the look out for some bonus events happening around the hotel. You could win something very special. The rest of the day is yours, I'm sure you are all tired from travelling. The first session begins tomorrow at 9 a.m. sharp."

Dr Patrick quickly exited the room, offering no opportunity for Sam to ask the myriad of questions rattling around his head.

"Well, that was weird," said the boy next to him.

Sam smiled, but didn't know how to respond. The boy offered his hand.

"Kyle Anderson," he said with a grin.

Sam shook his hand. He knew the name - it was at the top of the leader board. Typical.

"Sam Rayner. Your accent, is it American?"

"I'm from San Diego. Parents work over here." He looked around and lowered his voice. "Don't you think this is all, y'know, a little suspicious?"

When Sam looked around he realised that they were the only two still sitting. The other players were walking out with only a few of them talking, the rest remained silent and looked unfriendly. The atmosphere was competitive but Sam couldn't see anything suspicious.

"Looks fine to me. And the chance to play games for money is brilliant!"

"Who's sponsoring all of this?"

Sam shrugged. "Does it matter?"

"That's what they want you to think."

"Who are 'they'?"

Kyle's eyes narrowed as he sized Sam up. "What game did you play to get here?"

"Code One on my handheld. "

"And you think you were really the first person to complete it? Code One's been out for a few months."

Sam felt suddenly defensive. Was this Kyle's trick to make him doubt his own skills? Was it a ploy to wear down his opponent's morale?

"Well obviously I was. Or I had the highest score."

"I was playing Flashzone on my Xbox when I got the message. Next day the phone rings with an invite to this."

"That happened to me. I bet it happened to everyone here."

"See, the thing is, I never gave Flashzone my phone number, name or address. How did they know where to find me?"

Sam was about to respond when he suddenly realised the same thing had happened to him. How had they got his details?

"Another thing," Kyle continued

conspiratorially, "I checked it out online; this competition happens all around the world, in a different country each time."

"So?"

"So there are reports of kids taking part who vanish."

"Vanish? You mean they give up because they're too low on the scoreboard to win?"

"Quitting is the official reason they suddenly left. I think they were taken by a shadowy organisation."

Sam eyed the door. Kyle was between him and it. The boy was clearly a nutter.

Kyle continued: "Think about it. We've all got above-average reactions, attention to detail and problem solving skills. They're the skills that develop with the games we play."

"Then why not just turn up to the house and kidnap them without bothering to run this competition. Surely that would be more secretive?"

Kyle froze - that had clearly not occurred to him.

"And why take people who are not even close

41

to winning? The ones who are ready to quit?" pressed Sam. "Surely the winner would be more useful for... for whatever evil plan you think they're being used for." Kyle stared into space with glazed eyes as if he was daydreaming. Sam stood up and feigned a yawn.

"Well, I'm tired. I better get an early night if I'm going to win this thing."

That caused Kyle to snap back to the conversation.

"Good luck. You'll really need it to beat me!"

Sam grinned and headed for the door. That was a more normal reaction. When he reached the door he glanced back. Kyle had made no attempt to leave and was sitting alone in the room staring at the names on the scoreboard. He glanced over at Sam.

"Remember, keep your eyes peeled," said Kyle before focusing back on the board.

Peeled for what? thought Sam. Then he remembered - the bonuses Dr Patrick had mentioned! He wondered what they could be. He crossed the quiet lobby - then he noticed the sunglass-wearing man was still standing outside. Now it was dark, the man had pushed the sunglasses to rest on top of his head.

He was angled away from the lobby, but Sam got the distinct impression that he was being watched. How much of their conversation had the man overheard?

He felt a chill as he recalled Kyle's warning. "Stupid..." he mumbled under his breath. That was directed at both himself for half-believing the story and to Kyle for prattling on about such nonsense. Returning to his room he found Rebecca had gone, leaving the place in the usual bomb site girls made.

A quick check next door revealed his parents were not there either. They must have gone for dinner and his stomach rumbled on cue. He returned to his own suite and found his mobile phone on the bed exactly where he had left it. He unlocked it, intending to ring his mum to find out where they were - but a new icon on the phone caught his attention. It was an eye surrounded by binary code. It certainly wasn't on it when he last looked.

He felt angry at the idea that his sister must have used his phone behind his back. Then he hesitated and his anger turned to curiosity. Was this one of the mysterious bonuses he was supposed to look out for? It could have been placed on his phone over the hotel's wireless network...

Curious, he tapped the icon. The eye widened as the digital pupil expanded and the program initiated. The screen flashed a rapid series of colours and a single word faded up: POLYBIUS.

CHAPTER FOUR
UNEXPECTED EVENTS

"Where have you been?" snapped Rebecca, arms akimbo and the usual frown on her face.

Sam entered the suite and blinked stupidly for a few seconds before finally remembering where he was.

"I came looking for you," he said. He glanced around the room wondering how he had got back here, or more importantly, when he'd left.

"Mum was worried. We saw all the other gamers had left the hall. She rang your mobile but it went straight to answer phone."

Sam tried to put the last half hour together. "I came up here after the briefing. I was hungry so I went down to find out if you were in the restaurant."

"We were! And that was two hours ago!"

"Two hours?" said Sam in surprise. He glanced

at his watch and, sure enough, it was later than he'd thought. "I... I..." He looked at his phone and suddenly remembered the new game he had found. "I was playing Polybius before I left. I must have been more tired than I thought." That triggered a big yawn as he spoke which made the last few words unintelligible.

Rebecca rolled her eyes. "I have no idea how to speak geek. What's Polybius?"

"It's a game I found on my phone. You didn't download it, did you?" he said suspiciously.

"I never touched your stupid phone!" They had had so many arguments in the past over this that Sam was inclined to believe her. "We asked around and they said you were probably with that new friend of yours. Some boy you were talking to."

"Oh, Kyle? I was speaking to him before I came up." Sam tried to think back. Perhaps they had been talking longer than he had thought?

"Anyway, you better tell mum you're back."

Sam nodded. He was no longer feeling hungry but felt physically exhausted. He'd pop in on his parents and assure them he was fine, and then he planned to go straight to bed so he would feel refreshed for the competition tomorrow.

If he couldn't sleep, then there was always another game of Polybius he could cram in.

The next morning was the usual rush for Sam. He woke up late and charged out of bed, bypassing breakfast. He made it to the gaming hall, still tucking his t-shirt into his jeans, with seconds to spare. The other competitors were being seated by the same woman who had registered Sam the day before. He noticed that she still refused to smile. Dr Patrick stood next to the door with a tablet computer in his hands. Sam headed straight for him.

"Hi, I'm—"

"Sam Rayner," said Patrick without looking at his screen. "Being late for a game is an automatic forfeit. You are on machine twelve. Gail?" The icy woman studied Sam as if he were a scientific specimen. "Show Mr Rayner to his seat."

She led Sam to his seat without saying a single word. The screen showed a racing game he was unfamiliar with. He put on his headset and moved the mouse over the range of vehicles he could drive. His head banged from a headache that had been with him since the moment he had awoken. He hadn't managed to get very much sleep and was feeling just as tired as the night before. On top of that, he was usually appalling at racing games so the competition had started with his weakest skill.

Sam picked a vehicle and was selecting the bodywork style when the screen suddenly flashed through a series of colours. It happened quickly and Sam was vaguely aware of a series of large letters and symbols appearing for microseconds.

He blinked and rubbed his eyes. The racing game was back. Looking around the room he couldn't tell if anybody else had experienced the same phenomena. Certainly nobody was reacting if they had. The symbols seemed vaguely familiar. Had he seen them in the Polybius game?

Dr Patrick spoke up. "You have thirty seconds to customise your vehicles then the race will begin. You are all racing against one another but there can only be one winner!"

Sam spotted Kyle across the room from him. He was rubbing his eyes. Their gaze met for a second and Sam felt as though Kyle could read his thoughts and knew exactly what Sam had just seen. Sam shook his head; that was just paranoid nonsense from the conversation they had the night before.

"Ready to race!" shouted Dr Patrick.

Sam's car was suddenly on the start grid, the course ahead was an uneven rally track. He scrambled for the mouse knowing that he'd made several rookie mistakes. He had chosen completely the wrong car and he had spent too much time customising his vehicle rather than learning the controls.

The race lights turned green and several cars sped from the line. Sam was relieved to see most of the other players had fallen in the same trap and the hall was filled with the sounds of keys being randomly pressed in desperate attempts to get started.

Sam's engine revved as he hit the 'A' key, and suddenly he was in the race. The rough terrain and the ill-suited vehicle he had chosen resulted in a terrible lap time, but at least he didn't come last.

"Oliver Corvy, congratulations on winning that bout," Dr Patrick announced.

Sam looked around and saw Oliver, who wore a

smug smile that irritated everybody around him.

"You have a five minute break before round two."

The symbols that had flashed on his screen still burned in Sam's brain. When he screwed up his eyes, he could still see them.

He reached for his phone in his pocket to make a note of the letters in case they meant something - but was dismayed to find he had left it in the room again.

He hoped Rebecca wasn't touching it because he had racked up a high score on Polybius when he couldn't sleep and had been forced to pause the game just to rest. It was a simple tunnel-running shoot-'em-up game, the type that never normally interested him, but he had been hooked because of the subtle puzzle element woven between every turn he made. It was fiendishly addictive and he had played it for most of the night which was why he was now so tired.

"Round two is loaded!" declared Dr Patrick.

Sam blinked. He must have been daydreaming for the last few minutes. He caught Dr Patrick staring at him with the intensity of a headmaster. Sam's cheeks burned with embarrassment, he didn't want the doctor to think he wasn't serious about the competition - but with being late, daydreaming and performing so badly, he was surely giving that impression.

The new game that appeared on screen was a more familiar first person futuristic combat game, although, like the racing game, he had never played it before. Sam suspected that every game in the competition was specially made. This time Sam headed straight for the instructions, and committed the keys to memory.

The game was fast and furious and Sam played exceptionally well. He made it through to the last three players before his character was killed. A boy on the table next to him was pronounced winner. Sam looked at the leader board and suddenly realised how impossibly-difficult the competition was. Two boys had a point each, while everybody else was on zero. Sam felt cheated that his third place hadn't earned him anything.

And that's how the rest of the day progressed. Twelve unfamiliar games in total - playing almost every genre Sam could think of, with only a brief lunch break, during which Sam sat quietly with Kyle, who also complained of a headache.

Dr Patrick and the humourless Gail intently watched every game on the master monitor without ever looking up at the players themselves. During one game he noticed they were quietly arguing and, as Dr Patrick walked away, Gail treated him to a hostile look. Then she turned straight to Sam. Her gaze was so intense that Sam suddenly and unexpectedly felt frightened at being caught eavesdropping rather than playing the game. He continued the game, but performed terribly.

By the end of the day there were twelve separate people on the scoreboard with a single point each. Kyle was one of them, which annoyed Sam further because he was still on zero despite several near-wins.

With the tournament over for the day, Sam and Kyle walked back to their rooms.

"That was weird, eh?" said Kyle.

"Not really. Well done for winning a point. I've got nothing."

"I don't think it's about the points," said Kyle in a low voice. He glanced around - then suddenly pulled Sam's arm. His grip was so strong Sam felt his arm go numb.

"OW!"

"Ssshh! Look!"

Sam followed Kyle's gaze to the mysterious black suited sunglass wearing man from the day before sitting in the lobby reading a newspaper. At least this time he wasn't wearing the shades, but he looked suspicious nevertheless.

"Did you see him try to come into the hall earlier?" whispered Kyle.

"No."

"That Gail woman chased him out before he could have a good look. I've seen him lurking around since I arrived."

"He looks sus," admitted Sam. "But he's probably just a guest otherwise they would have thrown him out of the hotel. "Don't forget, your President has stayed here. They know how to do security."

Kyle continued walking. "And did you see the way Dr Patrick and Gail were staring at their screens the whole time and arguing?"

"Well it's a bit more interesting watching the

game than watching us."

"Something's not right. I can feel it."

They stopped outside Kyle's room. He drew his key card and used it to point at Sam. "Let me know if you see anything out of the ordinary, OK?"

Sam sighed and nodded. "OK. See you tomorrow." He quickly headed for his room. "Weirdo," he mumbled under his breath.

The maid had thoroughly tided the room, which was a relief because, while Sam was messy, his sister made the room look as though a tornado had struck it.

"Hello?"

No answer. Rebecca was out, which meant his parents would be making the most of the luxuries the hotel had to offer. He searched for his phone to call them, but couldn't find it. Apart from his book, the bedside drawer was empty as was his coat pocket. Peeking under the bed revealed nothing there. Sam's puzzlement began to give way to irritation as he continued searching. The only thing he found was a pencil and a single metal hairgrip his sister used. He absently pocketed both.

Either his sister had taken his phone or somebody had stolen it, which he doubted.

There was a sudden knock at the door.

Sam hurried to answer. "If you've forgotten your key..."

He swung the door open expecting to see Rebecca - but instead saw a sharp black suit and his own reflection in a pair of menacing shades. Sam's reaction was instantaneous—

SLAM! He forced the door closed with as much force as he could muster. He heard it crack against the man's nose and a groan of pain. But the door didn't shut - the man had wedged his shoe in between the gap.

Sam shouldered the door again - at the exact same time that the man did. The adult's greater weight won out - and Sam was flung across the room. He toppled over one of the sofas and crashed into the coffee table littered with tourist pamphlets. The wood cracked in half from the impact.

The man charged into the room. Sam shook his head, clearing the grogginess he felt since the door had struck him.

"Sam? Wait—" the man began as he reached out.

Once again Sam's accelerated reactions overtook his ability to rationalise the situation. He was on full fight mode.

The toes of his trainer hooked under the broken edge of the table and he kicked the wood at the man with every ounce of strength he had. The smashed coffee table struck the man across the head - and snapped his shades in half, as well as further crunching his nose.

Sam was stunned. The move was worthy of a martial arts champion and he never knew that he possessed such incredible reactions.

The man reeled backwards, clutching his nose and howling in pain. Sam was on his feet, instantly aware that he had to get around the intruder to escape. He searched for a weapon and snatched the table lamp. He pulled hard - wrenching the plug from the socket. By the time the man was ready to strike again, Sam was using the cord to whirl the lamp around his head like a cowboy's lasso.

"STOP!" shouted the man. His broken nose

made him sound like he was full of cold. "I'm on your side!"

"Get out of my room!" snarled Sam.

"I'm here to help you get your sister back!"

Sam hesitated - it was enough of a pause for the lamp to clatter to the ground. The man made no attempt to approach him. He held up his hands defensively.

"My name is Agent Jones," he said in an American accent. "You've been recruited by the SQA... and there has been a terrible mix up."
Sam squinted at him suspiciously. He nodded for Jones to continue.

"Your sister has been abducted by enemy agents and now the fate of our spy network hangs by a thread. Sam, we need your help!"

CHAPTER FIVE
THE WRONG RECRUIT

Ice cubes cracked as Agent Jones pressed a plastic bag full of them against his nose to combat the swelling.

Sam had allowed him to open the room's minibar, which was a fridge located under the desk. A small freezer compartment was packed with ice, and Agent Jones had scooped it all out.

"I don't understand," said Sam as he sat on the sofa opposite the injured man. This time, Sam positioned himself near the door, ready for a quick escape. He had done so automatically, and only later marvelled at his forward planning. It was most unlike him.

"Polybius is the key," said Jones.

"You mean the game I was playing?"

"Game?' the man laughed and shook his head.

"It's not a game. It's a sophisticated neural-enhanced training program designed to develop a new wave of spies."

Sam didn't understand, but laughed at the very idea. How could shooting robots in a tunnel train somebody to be a spy? Jones was ready with the answer.

"Yeah, I know how that sounds. The game has been around in some form or other since the eighties, before that they tried a whole bunch of recruitment schemes - including comics. It started as an arcade machine then, as home computers and consoles became more advanced, it appeared on those. Cell phones are the latest recruitment tools."

"Recruiting for this SQA? Who runs that? What is it?"

"The Spy Quest Agency. It was originally the brainchild of a crazy American-German scientist called Professor David Zimmerman. It identifies children at an early age who have an aptitude for espionage, spy-craft, that kind of thing. Then they would be recruited because they tended to make the best agents. Just like you."

"All because I'm good at a game?"

"Then don't think of it as a game. Polybius was developed to tune into those skills that are vital to spies. The program is designed to made this work," he tapped the side of his head, "to its ultimate potential. When Nathan Goucher became head of the SQA he appointed two new department heads: Nick Graham, Head of Training and Alex Carter our communications whiz. They developed the SQA in a variety of formats. Quest-based computer games, arcade games, lots of different variations and across computers, phones, the internet wherever they could - just so we could secretly place it in hotels, holiday parks, cruise ships and even schools. That way we can access the sharpest, brightest talent."

"OK. So, let's just pretend I believe all of that," said Sam, his brain racing to file away the torrent of information. "Why do all that in the first place?"

"Rather than Allied Governments wasting resources spying on each other, money was spent on attacking our collective enemies. There are many sinister forces out there just waiting to overthrow countries like yours and mine, and I'm not just talking about rival governments. I'm talking about organized criminals, syndicates, dictators... crazy folk of all kind."

Hundreds of questions buzzed around Sam's head. "Why recruit kids?"

"Because you guys make incredible spies. You learn quickly, can be trained faster than an adult, your reaction times are sharper too. Plus, the enemy is less likely to suspect a child. Equally important is that the program uses subliminal messages..."

He noticed Sam's blank look.

"There are messages hidden away within the game. Things you won't consciously notice but your brain does. The images flash up very quickly and activities that happen in the background that you don't watch, because you are watching the action, but your eye sees it all. Your subconscious starts to learn without you ever realizing. Look how good your reflexes and combat skills have become, and that's only after a few hours training."

So, Kyle was on to something, Sam thought. Did Kyle know the truth or was he just guessing? Or...

"Doesn't that mean the enemy uses kids in their battles too?"

"Exactly right," said Jones as he repositioned the

ice pack on his nose.

"So the other competitors here...?"

"Some of them could be enemy agents, yes."

Sam was quiet for a moment. There was a lot he wanted to know about the SQA, but there was the more pressing matter of his sister's whereabouts and whether he should trust Agent Jones at all.

"OK. Supposing I believe you. How do I know which side you're on?"

Jones wagged his finger. "That's a good question, and exactly why you were chosen. I'm on the side looking to rescue your sister."

"And that's my next question. Why would anybody want to kidnap her?"

"Because they think she is you!" Jones rose from his seat and moved to the French windows, peering out into the darkness beyond. He glanced at his watch.

"Me? Why would they think that?"

"She got the highest score ever on Polybius."

Sam felt his heart sink. He had been playing that game. He'd paused the action to try and sleep. Rebecca had obviously been snooping on his phone and continued playing the game when she'd found his phone.

"Um... I think that was my score," he said defensively.

Jones chuckled. "I know. But the enemy doesn't. They think she is the best spy the SQA has ever produced. This program has been set up across the globe to recruit people just like that. Re-launching Polybius was an experiment of mine that has now... gotten out of hand."

Sam was annoyed that Rebecca had managed to steal his fame, but his anger quickly faded when he remembered she might be in danger.

"Who's taken her? Where is she?"

Jones looked at his watch again. "As to who has taken her, I don't know. We have many enemies, but one thing is clear - SQA has a mole, a Double Agent working inside the organisation. That's who took your sister. As to where she is - I think it highly likely she's already on her way out of the country."

"We need to tell the police!" said Sam and leapt from his chair to reach the telephone on the desk. He raised the handset, his finger hovering over the keypad.

"And tell them what? They won't take a missing

person seriously unless it has been over twenty-four hours and right now you have no proof she has been abducted. By then it will be too late. They will have reprogrammed her brain, wiping her memories of you, your parents. She will become an enemy spy... and if they discover she is not the Polybius champion they think she is, they are more than likely to kill her - then come looking for you."

Sam slowly replaced the phone. His hand was shaking; the reality of the situation frightened him.

"Why don't we call my phone? She might still have it?"

"Because then we lose the element of surprise. Right now her kidnappers don't know that we're on to them. Let's keep it that way. I suspect the moment we leave here there will be somebody following us, but the less we give away our intentions, the better."

Sam looked around the room.

"There maybe a clue as to who took her?"

Jones smiled and nodded. "Now you're thinking like a spy. The problem is housekeeping has been in here already and will have destroyed any evidence."

"Plus I bet they used a whole bunch of hi-tech

gadgets, just like James Bond. Do we get any?"

"Gadgets are a lot of fun, but let's face it, computers can be hacked, phones lost. The art of real spying still uses the old school methods. Secret codes, drop boxes... you name it." He noticed the disappointed look on Sam's face. "But we still have some surprises."

Sam studied the room. Every book he'd read, game he'd played or film he'd watched had so many elements of sophisticated code breaking technology that he had to think hard to recall an old "how to be a spy" handbook he had once taken from the library. People were so technology focused they tended to ignore the most obvious things...

His eyes fell onto a small notepad at the edge of the desk. It bore the hotel's logo, but the room's light revealed subtle shadows on the white paper. They were indentations created as somebody had written on the top sheet, then torn the page out. He hadn't used the pad... had Rebecca tried to leave a message?

Sam took the pencil he had pocketed and used the broad side of the point to rub over the furrows. Sure enough it revealed writing:

9.359

Sam blinked. That was meaningless. Agent Jones peered over his shoulder and gasped.

"Brilliant, Sam!"

"I have no idea what that means."

"I do. We need a radio."

"There's one in the car..."

"No a real old one capable of receiving shortwave stations."

Sam thought hard. He was sure he'd seen one recently...

"In the lobby!" he exclaimed. "There is an old one used as an ornament."

"Go get it," ordered Jones.

It took several minutes for Sam to return with the old wooden radio. It was rather heavy, but he had been able to snatch it away when the receptionist had been distracted. He had wasted a little time to check that Rebecca wasn't in the restaurant with their parents. Seeing his mum and dad eating together had helped confirm part of Jones' incredible story.

Jones took the radio as soon as Sam entered the room. He placed it on the desk and plugged it in. The old set wheezed to life. Jones selected the shortwave setting and used a chunky dial to scrub through the channels in a cacophony of whines, whistles, static and occasional snatches of music and voices. He settled on 9.359 Mhz. An awful nursery rhyme tune played. It sounded ancient and Sam thought that it must have been played on an old organ of some kind.

"It's only the first few bars of the song repeating over and over," noted Sam. "What kind of rubbish radio station is this?"

"We call them number stations. They're everywhere, you've just got to listen. Intelligence agencies from around the world use them to relay messages to spies. It can't be traced or intercepted like emails or text messages and nobody needs special equipment to listen in. The old ways really are sometimes the best."

Before Sam could ask his next question a voice started speaking on the radio. It was a woman's voice, but it sounded unusual, a computer simulation of a voice. She began reading numbers in a monotonous rhythm. Jones hurriedly wrote them down.

"33, 15, 53, 44, 15, 45, 42, 34, 43, 44, 11, 42, 44, 34, 35, 11, 42, 24, 43, 21, 24, 42, 43, 44, 14, 15, 13, 25, 15, 24, 21, 21, 15, 31, 32, 24, 14, 14, 11, 54, 21, 34, 42, 33, 15, 45, 42, 11, 31, 13, 23, 24, 35," droned the voice.

Sam was confused. None of it made sense. He patiently waited for the message to stop, then the nursery rhyme began again and Jones turned the radio off and stared at the mass of numbers on the page.

"That code will keep repeating for a couple of hours. Since whoever took your sister knew exactly which station to listen to, this code was meant for them."

They looked at the incomprehensible chain of numbers.

"What does it mean?"

Agent Jones was thoughtful for a long moment. "It's difficult. Without the key to crack the code..." He shook his head, and then noticed the look of despair on Sam's face when he realised the only lead they had to track down his sister was a nonsense jumble of numbers.

Jones continued. "I said it's difficult, but not

impossible. With codes you need to look for repeated letters. Like these elevens, they're probably vowels." He lapsed into silence again, and then he finally sighed and rubbed his eyes. "I don't know..."

Sam paced the room, aware that every wasted moment took his sister further away.

"This whole operation would have to be planned for a long time, right?"

Jones shook his head. "Not necessarily. The SQA recruitment drive was well known, but the idea to put the Polybius app out there was only made yesterday. For somebody to have found out about it, and then monitored the game, they would have had to have operated quickly and improvised everything. Otherwise they wouldn't have been so clumsy as to leave that indentation on your writing pad."

"In that case, this code isn't something they would have had time to set up. It would have to be something basic, especially if it was all spur of the moment?"

Agent Jones froze. He looked at Sam with wide eyes. "You may just have cracked it, Sam!"

"I did?"

Jones was already drawing a grid on the page filled with numbers.

"You're right. This whole operation to abduct the best Polybius player was spur of the moment. Whoever the SQA mole is they would not have had time to develop a specific code for the operation. If they had to improvise a code, they would have used the most obvious one to save time and confusion with their command centre. The Polybius code it the obvious choice!"

He showed Sam the grid he been working on.

	1	2	3	4	5
1	A	B	C	D	E
2	F	G	H	I/J	K
3	L	M	N	O	P
4	Q	R	S	T	U
5	V	W	X	Y	Z

"It was a Greek scholar named Polybius who first developed this idea of encrypting messages into a code. It's a basic encryption, but something you could use in a hurry! I'll read out the number, you decode the letter. The first number reads down, the next one, across."

Jones began reading the numbers in the same monotonous way the artificial voice on the radio had. This time he split them into single digits - three, three instead of thirty-three...

"33," became N

"15," became E

"53," became X

"44," became T

Sam's eyes widened as the letters he was deciphering suddenly made sense. He didn't understand the entire message but one thing was for sure... he no longer doubted Agent Jones.

CHAPTER SIX
THE CHASE IS ON

Sam tried to sleep but his mind was racing too fast and he kept wriggling in the uncomfortable car seat. He glanced at Agent Jones who gripped the steering wheel as he intently peered through the windscreen.

They had left the hotel almost instantly. Agent Jones had accompanied Sam to visit his parents who were still eating in one of the many restaurants. Jones had conjured up a quick cover story that Sam was leading the way in the tournament so they might not see much of him over the next few days. They seemed fine with the notion, and Sam even added that Rebecca had made some new friends so would be doing her own thing. He was relieved to notice that his parents were thrilled with the notion of not seeing their children for the next few days. Worried parents were an extra pressure he didn't need right now.

"More time for you and dad to spend in the spa," said Sam with a fake smile.

That had gone down well and, as they left the hotel, Agent Jones was confident they had two days to save Rebecca and return to the hotel before the alarm was raised. Sam felt guilty for lying - which was a first as it had never bothered him before. But this time, with genuine deadly stakes, it played on his conscience.

Now they had left Scotland and were speeding down the backbone of England in a race to catch up with the enemy agent. Jones had warned him that they had a good eight hour journey ahead of them, seven if he broke a few speeding laws, but Sam doubted the old car was capable of that. He had been expecting a cool spy car, an Aston Martin or something, but instead Jones drove a rusty heap of junk.

"Easier to blend in," he had told Sam.

Unable to sleep, Sam took the opportunity to air the questions that were still plaguing him.

"I still don't understand why they would kidnap the best Polybius player. Doesn't the enemy have their own recruitment games?"

"Right now we don't know which enemy is behind all this. But I suspect the message may have hinted at that. The Neural Chip is a clue."

"I have no idea what that is," said Sam. When they decoded the message he thought he had written the wrong word down, but Jones had assured him he was correct.

"Polybius works by hiding images within the game. Shapes and codes are hidden in plain sight. You don't see them but your brain does."

"That doesn't make any sense."

"Okay... have you ever lost something, like a pen, or your phone, and searched everywhere for it - only to eventually find it right under your nose?"

"All the time. When it happens I think I must be getting old."

Jones laughed and shook his head. "Well you can relax. That's perfectly normal. Your brain is more advanced than any computer and it has to process a lot of information - what you see, smell, touch, feel, hear - all at the same time. To do that it takes a few shortcuts and only shows you what you expect to hear or see. So when you play the game images flash up so quickly that your brain decides that you don't need to see them because they're not relevant to the action on screen." Sam frowned, but it sort of made sense. "So my attention isn't drawn to the weird flashes, even though I have seen them."

"Yes. And the information is still absorbed in your mind in the background. That's what subliminal means. That way we are able to train you with new skills, without you being aware of it."

"That's why I reacted so fast when you entered the room?"

Jones nodded and touched his sore nose. "And we're able to teach you martial arts skills you had never learnt before."

"Sorry about that," mumbled Sam apologetically.

"That's fine. Shows your training is working - and remember that every game you played in the competition was testing you. They were like real-world instruction books. How to fight, how to drive, how to break codes - they were all specially designed to make your unconscious mind learns new skills."

"That's why the games were all so different!"

"Exactly! So, the Neural Chip was created by a brilliant scientist who went straight into hiding after he drummed up a lot of bad gambling debts. Word on the black market is that he's willing to sell the chip to anybody who can prove it will work. It works in a similar way to Polybius except rather than train your brain over time it reprograms it immediately. It replaces your personality forever. The old you is gone, and the new you is essentially a living robot, doing whatever it's ordered to do. Overnight you would become an expert spy... and a completely different person."

"That doesn't sound too bad."

"Really? Imagine you were programmed to hate your sister... okay, bad example. What about turning you into somebody who hated computer games and crisps and was more into gardening?"

"That would be horrible."

"And what if, as well as gardening, I could make you obey any instruction I gave you? Like go and hit the Prime Minister with a shovel - and you were unable to ever resist?" Sam nodded as the implications sank in. "The problem is it's experimental technology, so, of course, it doesn't work properly. The SQA abandoned it years ago, but a small group of rogue spies, codenamed Oblivion, have been trying to get their hands on the technology to create their own army of super-agents. They don't work for any one government and have their own dangerous agenda."

"But why Rebecca... or rather, why me?"

"Because a Polybius Agent's brain has been perfectly conditioned so that it is more receptive to brainwashing. Usually Neural Chip test subjects have seizures and die, but the theory is that Polybius would have prepared your brain for a complete personality transplant. But it has never been tested.

"Nobody has anything as good as Polybius. The competition back at Glendevon has been used as an open day for security services around the world to pick the best possible agents. I can assure you that the hotel was crawling with enemy agents, and some friendly ones too - all trying to identify the best candidates. It is impossible to block every enemy out."

"Huh, then that rules me out as a best candidate. I didn't score a single point."

"Winning is not about getting the most points."

"Since when?"

Jones glanced at him, only daring to take his eyes off the road for a second.

"What the games prove is that somebody is good at racing while somebody else has the speed and dexterity to line up targets and shoot them. A third person is a great problem solver. You know what they all have in common?"

"They're winners?" said Sam glumly.

"They're only good at one thing. SQA is looking for recruits who are good at everything. That usually means successful candidates never come first in any one discipline. Do you know how well you were scoring?"

"No."

"Across the board you were scoring brilliantly."

Sam felt a sudden rush of confidence. The compliment washed away the fatigue he was feeling.

"So you think I would have made it as a spy?"

"You are top of the list, Sam. And as of right now, you really are a spy. SQA instructed that I bring you along to find your sister. Now with a mole in the camp, and the Neural Chip program being reactivated... I need all the assistance I can get."

"Cool!" Sam glanced at his reflection in the

sun visor's mirror, imagining himself as James Bond. Somehow he didn't quite look like the hero type. He flipped the visor back up and studied Agent Jones curiously.

"How did you become a spy? Did you always want to be one?"

He noticed Jones' hands gripped the wheel tighter but his gaze never left the road.

"You should try and rest," said Jones enigmatically. "We have a lot of distance to cover."

Sam wondered why Jones was so reluctant to talk about his own experiences. He watched the road endlessly twist and turn ahead. One thing was for sure, he wouldn't be falling asleep.

Five minutes later, Sam was fast asleep.

When Sam awoke he was still in the car but unsure where they were. The car was parked in what looked, at first glance, to be a swaying garage. There was a car parked in front and behind. Agent Jones was still in the driver's seat, his brow knitted in concentration. He was so focused that he flinched when Sam spoke up.

"Where are we?"

"On the Eurotunnel. We've just left England."

Sam had never been on the Eurotunnel before and had expected a futuristic train. It looked like they had just parked in a normal train carriage, the only difference being that there were no seats.

"We've had a tail since I stopped for gas on the highway." Jones never taking his eyes from the mirrors.

"Who's following us?"

"Maybe the SQA mole, or their sidekick. Do you suspect anybody?"

Sam thought for a moment. "That Kyle boy was a bit weird. And Dr Patrick was always giving me the evil eye."

"Patrick is a good man, one of the senior people at SQA. I can't believe he would turn traitor. What about that man in the kilt, remember him?"

Sam nodded. "And he directed me to the wrong room on the first day. Does that count as sabotage?"

"Wait here and lock the doors."

Jones quickly got out of the car and walked towards the rear of the train. Sam watched him in the mirror, but quickly lost sight of him as he passed through a dividing fire door into another carriage behind. Sam couldn't see anybody acting suspiciously. There was nobody in the car behind and the driver of the one in front looked old and was sleeping.

Just as Sam was beginning to think Jones was being overly suspicious the carriage door ahead of him opened and a large bald man stepped through. He was huge, his clothes barely fitting the muscular arms beneath, and the sleeves stopping short halfway up his wrists. He looked as menacing as Frankenstein's monster and gave Sam a toothy smirk.

Sam felt a shiver of fear. This man was obviously no agent; there was nothing secretive about him. He was a man of violence and it showed across his mean face.

"Hello, little man. Boris has found you." His accent was a thick eastern European one and made the sentence sound even more sinister.

The thug calling himself Boris held a small spray canister in his hand and quickly blasted the paint over the small recessed security camera in the corner. The small blue paint stain was enough to hide the punishment he was about to administer on Sam. Boris glanced at the slumbering driver in the car ahead and causally advanced on Sam.

Sam was paralysed with fear. There was no way he was a physical match for the monster and a quick glance around the car revealed no weapons. Sam honked the horn hoping it would get Jones' attention but the horn just echoed around the carriage and failed to wake the sleeping driver. The rattle of the train around him swallowed the noise and he doubted that it could be heard in the adjacent carriages.

Boris was now at the front of the car and pushed down on the bonnet - shaking the vehicle with a single hand. The thug's eyes screwed up to tiny points of malice as he rushed for Sam's door. With a sense of dread, Sam realised that he had forgotten Jones' instruction to lock the door.

Sam's hand snapped out for the door lock - just as Boris grabbed the handle and pulled!

Luckily Sam's reflexes were sharp and the lock fell with a satisfying THUD. Boris yanked on the door so hard that he pulled the metal handle straight off! Sam knew that must have taken incredible strength and it made him feel even more vulnerable trapped inside the vehicle. Sam tried to quell his mounting panic -

surely he was safe? Even if it was old, the car had been designed to absorb high-speed crashes—

SMASH! Sam jumped as the side window next to his head suddenly fractured. Boris had punched through it and showed no sign of pain as he raised his fist for another strike...

"Boris gonna get you, little man!"

BAM! The whole window turned white as the glass fractured - but didn't break. The safety glass held, but bent like a stiff rubber sheet, obscuring Sam's view of the brute. He had no doubt the next impact would break through.

Sam clambered for the back seat - but was yanked backwards by his seatbelt! He had forgotten to take it off! His fingers scrambled for the belt release as a hole was punched through the glass - a huge fist narrowly missing Sam's head.

Sam's left hand found the seat's reclining lever. He fell flat on his back as the seat folded and Boris's hand groped to tear his face off. Sam crawled free of the still-fastened seatbelt and climbed onto the back seat.

The roving hand failed to connect with him and

*SMASH! Sam jumped as the side
window next to his head suddenly fractured.*

instead plucked the door lock open. Sam had a single second to think. The passenger door was opening and then his attacker would be in the car in seconds. The rear door was Sam's only escape route but that would put him outside where he'd be an exposed target. Somehow, he needed to weaken his attacker...

Sam booted the door the same moment Boris pulled it open. The brute hadn't been expecting the move and Sam heard the horrible crunch as the edge of the door struck the thug across the head. Boris staggered against the carriage wall.

It had bought Sam a few more precious moments and he was certain it had enraged Boris further. Sam partially opened the rear door and positioned himself to jump - but Boris shot through the passenger door like a Jack in the box!

Sam tried to leap out of the rear door - but a firm hand gripped his trainer and pulled him back inside. Boris was dragging him from the vehicle with ease!

Sam's fingers raked across the upholstery - then his trainer suddenly came off! The brute toppled backwards again and Sam crawled back to the rear seat. When he looked up again, Boris was on his feet and running around the front of the car, obviously intending a different angle of attack.

The train suddenly slowed and Sam could feel momentum was pushing him sharply forward. At that moment he was glad he'd paid attention in physics class. He leaned forward, gripped the car's handbrake and plunged it down–

The car rolled forward as the train rapidly decelerated. Boris cried out as the front bumper crushed his legs, pinning him against the car in front. The impact was enough to finally wake the old driver who looked wildly around in alarm.

Agent Jones suddenly ran into the carriage and sprang for Boris. Jones had the element of surprise and knocked the ogre out with a single slug across the chin. He looked at Sam but couldn't say anything before the old driver was out of his car and, in French, was loudly questioning what was going on.

Sam was buzzing from the affects of the adrenaline, which was now coursing through his body after the fight. He heard Jones improvise an excuse that their "friend" had simply been looking under the bonnet and had lightly nudged the man's car. With no damage to complain about the old man returned to his vehicle as the train's automatic P.A. system announced they were approaching Calais.

Agent Jones got back into his car and quickly brushed the broken glass off the passenger seat and into the footwell where he covered it over with the floor mat so that, with a casual glance, the border security wouldn't think anything was amiss. He gave back Sam's trainer and looked at him with concern.

"Are you OK?"

Sam nodded. He was trembling now the event was finally over.

"You've got the shakes. Try one of these." Jones handed him a chewy sweet. "Sugar will help. I shouldn't have left you alone, sorry about that."

Sam finally found his voice. "Who was he?"

"Our mole's hired muscle. I guess he was instructed to stop us at all costs. Good job I arrived in time or he would have killed you."

Sam shivered at the thought that he was so close to death. He also felt annoyed that Jones considered he'd saved the day, when Sam had won most of the fight through his own cunning.

"Your Polybius score was extraordinary, and since they think your sister got that score, they'll assume she will make an astonishing agent and the perfect candidate for whatever they plan with the Neural Chip. To them, it is well worth a few lives to recruit her."

"Rebecca's not stupid," Sam was thankful there was nobody else around to hear that admission, "She won't work for the bad guys."

"It's not always obvious who the bad guys are. They could easily convince her that she's working for the greater good or they could always threaten her. Besides, that doesn't matter since they're planning to erase her brain and start all over again. If we can stop them from getting the Neural Chip, we can derail their plans."

Sam didn't say anything. He had just experienced the ruthless side of what he had previously assumed was an exciting adventure. He looked around, "Where did Boris go?"

Agent Jones smiled and nodded towards the car in front. "When the old man opens his boot, he's in for a surprise!"

"Shouldn't we have searched him? Questioned him?"

"No point in interrogating a man like that. They're trained to withstand torture. And I did search him." Jones held up a mobile phone. A text message was on screen - once again a jumble of numbers, but this time they were all zeroes and ones. Sam read the first few lines. It was another code:

01101001011011100111010001100101011100100
10001101100101011100000111010100

Agent Jones sighed heavily. Exhaustion was finally showing on his face. "It might be nothing more than coordinates or instructions about stopping us, but see if you can make anything from it."

The train had come to a halt and the fire doors separating the carriages automatically lifted. Jones started the engine in anticipation.

"Aren't you worried he'll talk when he finally comes around?"

"Are you suggesting we... silence him?"

It took a moment for the implication to sink in - and Sam was horrified. "No, no, no! Not kill him, just... um..."

"It's almost impossible stopping somebody from talking, at least if it's not permanent. He'll squeal to his bosses no matter what. The best we can do is hope we're very far from him when he does wake up."

"And what makes you think the driver in front isn't heading for Paris too?"

"Belgium license plate. Odds are that he's heading home. Observation, that's the skill every successful spy has."

Sam stared at the smashed passenger window. *That and a whole lot of luck*, he silently added.

CHAPTER SEVEN
PARIS

As they passed through the passport control in Calais, Sam was suddenly aware that Agent Jones was using false passports. He tossed Sam's new identity into his lap as they pulled away. Sam read it with a grin.

"Carl Spironi?"

"First rule of spy-club: never use your real identity. It's the most precious thing you possess. Always use an alias in real life, just like online. The less people know about the real you, the better."

"So Jones isn't your real name?"

Jones smiled. "Today I'm your father, Tim Spironi. But you can call me dad."

"We sound more like the mafia!"

"You're privately educated in England, hence the accent. Try and put on a slight American twang tocomplete the cover. We're heading to Paris for a couple of days vacation together while I'm over on business. I work in software, your mother ran off when you were young that's why she's not here. You're an only child. Any questions?"

Sam examined his passport closely. His photo was very recent and there was nothing that indicated it was a fake.

"How did you get this made?"

"Remember when you signed in at the tournament? Gail Torrez is our recruitment officer. She got your picture, biometrics, fingerprints, everything the moment you signed in."

"Wow. That's... scary. The idea that they can get so much information about me."

"Oh, the SQA knows everything about you, Sam. You have no secrets from us."

Sam felt uncomfortable. "Not everything—"

"Everything! I read your file."

Sam thought it best not to provoke Jones in revealing just how much he knew, just in case any embarrassing facts came out. Instead he turned the conversation back to the agent.

"You still haven't told me exactly who the SQA are. Who am I working for? The Government?"

"Yes."

Sam waited for more details, but it was clear Jones was being tight-lipped. Whether it was because secrecy was important or Jones just didn't know, Sam couldn't tell. He changed tact.

"So how did they recruit you? Did you apply for the job? What made you want to become a spy?"

Jones looked askance, his eyes narrow. "You sure ask a lot of questions."

"And I don't get any answers..." mumbled Sam.

No further conversation took place. Agent Jones' gaze held on the road and he eyed each passing car with suspicion.

Sam noticed the time. It was very late - or rather very early in the morning. It would soon be light and any sign of tiredness had fled since he was attacked. He couldn't sleep with the knowledge that his sister was out there and in trouble.

He tucked the passport into his pocket and turned his attention to his attacker's mobile phone and the coded text message. After a minute of trying to see a pattern the solution suddenly struck him. He accessed the Internet through the phone and found a specific website. He loaded in the code.

"Got it! He proudly announced."

"Really? How?"

Sam read from the screen: "Intercept Rayner boy at all costs. Eliminate. Rendezvous..." he struggled with the pronunciation of the next part, "Sacre Coeur de Montmartre... after chip exchange."

Jones was impressed. "How...?"

"Binary! Zeroes and ones, the language of computers. In groups of six they represent letters, numbers, symbols. 01100001 is the letter 'A', that much I remember." Sam was pleased a useless fact had proven to be so important. "You should know this - the SQA logo is made up from binary. I just used a binary to text convertor on the web. Although I still don't understand what it means."

"Sacre Coeur de Montmartre is a church in Paris," said Jones thoughtfully. "The first code said they're meeting at the Eiffel Tower to obtain the Neural Chip. Once they have that they'll move quickly. The mole will have exposed their identity and they know we're not far behind. There must be something near the church... their headquarters, maybe? Whatever it is, we're running against the clock on this. We can't afford to make any mistakes - your sister's fate is in our hands. And if we fail, she'll be instrumental in creating an army of brainwashed agents... or she'll die in the attempt..."

They stopped at a rest area for more petrol and a few snacks. Agent Jones risked a thirty-minute power nap while Sam tried to stay awake, searching Boris's mobile for any information about their foes, but there was nothing. He'd even deleted the last number he'd called. With nothing to occupy him, Sam could no longer fight off sleep. Even as his eyelids shut, he could see a jumble of shapes and text flash against his eyelids...

Sam woke up to discover that Agent Jones had continued driving and was now parking in a quiet narrow street. Sam noted the buildings looked distinctly Parisian, or as much as he could judge from watching movies. It was also now raining heavily.

"Welcome to Paris," said Jones. "You slept

soundly. I hope you're feeling refreshed because we walk and take the subway from here on out."

Jones appeared to know his way around the Paris suburbs. He navigated the narrow streets at such a pace Sam was often running to catch up.

"Where are we going?" said Sam, trying to catch his breath and getting wetter with each step.

"An SQA safe house."

Sam jogged to keep up. "A what...?"

"Across the globe we use hotels and resorts as safe houses for all SQA agents. They make the perfect cover, they're always open and nobody bats an eyelid when strangers come and go."

Sam chuckled, thinking the idea sounded absurd. "That's..." but he stopped when he realised just how clever the SQA were being. Who would ever suspect a kid talking to a member of hotel staff? "That's brilliant!"

"And here we are," said Agent Jones gesturing to a discreet looking hotel. It was the kind of building easy to walk past without a second glance, unless you noticed the smartly dressed doorman standing just inside.

"Hôtel Whinfell V," said Sam reading the sign.

"If anything happens to me or we get separated, then you come here. Ask for Pierre, and give him the code word."

Jones entered the hotel, leaving Sam looking around for a street sign; he had no idea where they were. He finally spotted one.

"Avenue George V..." he repeated, before he recalled something else Agent Jones had said. "What do you mean 'if something happens to you'?" said Sam, running inside.

The hotel's interior was impeccably smart, with a thick carpet underfoot and shiny brass on the reception desk, doors and the sweeping banister leading to the floors above. Sam caught up with Agent Jones as he was speaking to a snooty looking man at reception. He guessed this was Pierre.

"I love Paris in the spring time," Jones said in a low voice.

The Receptionist didn't meet Jones' gaze, but his right eyebrow inched up in surprise. In flawless English he replied, "But the winter makes the city glow like a jewel." Then he disappeared into the back room. Jones indicated they should follow.

The paint on the walls of the narrow back corridor was peeling and the lights flickered. Hotel guests never got to see this part of the Whinfell.

Jones tapped a code on a small numeric keypad and a section of the wall suddenly slid away. Sam gasped; he could have sworn there was no door there.

They entered a small room filled with shelves containing stacks of laptops, phones, clothing and various metal cases. Pierre made himself busy selecting items off the shelf.

"What is this place?" whispered Sam.

"All SQA safe houses have a depot, a place where agents can get the equipment they need," Jones whispered back.

"Wow! Like super-gadgets and stuff like that?"

Jones gave him an odd look, then asked: "Why are you whispering?"

Before Sam could answer, Pierre handed Agent Jones a plastic bag and tapped the side of his nose in a gesture indicating they should keep quiet.

Before he had a chance to get dry, Sam found

himself following Agent Jones back in the rain.

"Pierre is a man of few words," Sam pointed out. When Agent Jones didn't say anything, Sam thought it best not to joke around any more.

They walked down several more streets, past a patisserie - the sweet smell of the cakes made Sam's stomach rumble - then down the steps of a Metro entrance. They were soon sitting on a rattling underground train, heading for a station called Passy.

"What we're about to do is incredibly dangerous," warned Jones. "We seldom expose Polybius trainees to this level of danger until they have had at least six months rigorous training. You'll need this." He handed a mobile phone to Sam.

Sam examined the device. It was much older than his own phone. His wild thoughts of cool spy gadgets were rapidly vanishing. "It's a bit... rubbish."

"If anything happens to me, that phone is your lifeline."

Sam was suddenly alarmed. "You keep saying that. What do you think is going to happen to you?"

"You never know. Just be prepared. For anything. Always keep your eyes open and your wits about you." He glanced at his watch. "We're on time."

Jones looked around the carriage. There were a few passengers at the opposite end: one read a newspaper while the other two talked loudly, their hands gesticulating to emphasise their points. Nobody was paying any attention to them. Jones rummaged in the plastic bag and withdrew a fake moustache. Sam giggled when he saw it.

"You don't expect me to wear that, do you?"

Agent Jones looked at him as if he were mad - then stuck the moustache underneath his own nose, using his reflection in the dark train window to position it. Then he extracted a pair of thick-framed glasses and a baseball cap.

"That's for you."

Sam took them with a frown. "What do I need these for?"

Jones rolled his eyes. "Think like a spy! They know what we look like. If we break up our appearance, even only a little, it will give us the edge. In this game, an edge is everything. Put them on."

Sam felt silly as he put them on, but had to admit his reflection already looked different. Jones pulled out a body warmer jacket and handed it to Sam.

"Stuff that on under your jacket, it'll make you look fatter. Keep your hands in your pockets as much as possible so nobody sees your skinny fingers. With any luck they won't notice you have a thin face. Any enemy agents will be looking out for a weedy kid."

"What about you? A moustache isn't exactly going to make you look that different."

"If we had more time there is a lot I could do to make me unrecognisable. But since time is against us, I'm going to have to wing it."

"I was expecting Pierre to give us something exciting. Something more useful than a plastic bag of junk."

Agent Jones shook his head and muttered under his breath. "Kids today... always wanting more." He stood up as they pulled into Passy station. "This is it."

They hurried out of the train and walked straight for the escalator. Agent Jones ran down the finer points of his plan, and gave Sam some tips on how to follow people without them noticing. He called it '*tailing*'. Sam tried to focus on every word, but his heart was beating hard in his chest. His sister lay somewhere ahead, probably terrified and he was about to embark on the most dangerous and bravest thing he had ever done in his life.

All the while, he could not help shake the feeling that he was far from ready...

The view across Paris from the first observation deck was impressive. Out, beyond the River Seine lay Paris' famous landmarks. Sam could see them all... on the postcard he held in his hands. He glanced out of the gift shop window but could see very little through the heavy leaden rainclouds. He would have loved to have seen more of the city, even more of the iconic steel tower he was standing on, but he had been instructed to head straight for the shop and wait for Agent Jones' signal.

Being a spy was a lot duller than he had imagined.

When they arrived, it had turned out that Passy was on the opposite side of the river from the Eiffel Tower and they had to cross the busy bridge, on different sides of the road from each other as enemy agents would be looking for a man and boy together.

Sam got his first look at the River Seine and the huge Eiffel Tower ahead, the top of which was lost in the low rain clouds.

Reaching the base of the tower, Jones purchased the admission tickets while Sam acted like the rest of the tourists and walked in a slow circle at the base of the tower, peering up and shielding his eyes from the rain. He'd made a single lap before Agent Jones bumped into him, approaching from the opposite direction. He mumbled an apology in French then hurriedly walked away as if they were strangers.

That was the plan. Jones had wanted to make sure the enemy hadn't seen them together. Sam's fingers went to his pocket and was surprised to feel the sharp edges of an admission ticket there. Jones was good - he had managed to plant it on Sam without him feeling a thing, and he had been expecting it! His fingers also fell on a tightly rolled bundle of Euros. How nice of Agent Jones to provide him with pocket money. He transferred the cash from his coat pocket to his jeans.

Sam passed through the entrance gate and queued up for the elevator. After ten minutes, in which he slowly shuffled towards the elevator, he finally found himself squashed between a dozen tourists in the elevator. It groaned and shook as it took them to the first floor deck.

Higher up, the wind was sharp, blowing the rain at an angle across the deck. Jones had told him to act casual and wait for the visual contact with his sister and her kidnapper. He took refuge from the storm in the gift shop, and peered through the rain blotched windows.

It didn't take long.

A girl was standing next to the rail; a baseball cap was the only protection from the elements. Sam tried to recall if he'd seen his sister wearing it before, but she had so many clothes that it was impossible to memorise them all. Her damp long black hair tumbled from the cap, masking her face. A figure stood at her side and Sam was certain he could see the stranger gripping the girl's shoulder as if to stop her running away. It was difficult to tell from behind and through a rain-smeared window, but Sam was certain it was Rebecca.

Who was the mysterious figure? Could it be Kyle? No, he was too small. Perhaps the kilted stranger in the hotel? Rain on the window made identification impossible.

Sam tried to innocently examine the souvenirs on display, but his heart was pounding once again. He kept Rebecca in view at all times, exactly as Jones had taught him. On more than one occasion Jones had warned him that the moment he lost visual contact with his target, he could lose her forever.

"Come on..." mumbled Sam impatiently. Surely Jones should have intercepted the kidnapper by now?

Precious seconds ticked by and there was still no sign of his mentor. Sam began to feel the icy grip of panic clutch his chest. Had something happened to Agent Jones?

The figure shoved Rebecca further along the edge of the deck, and Sam lost sight of them behind a thick steel lattice pillar that supported the tower. There was nowhere else to move in the shop, so Sam ran through the door, out into the rain.

Rebecca and her kidnapper had only moved a few metres into the corner of the observation platform where they examined one of many metal telescopes bolted to the deck that allowed visitors to view the panorama.

But there was still no sign of Jones.

Sam's fingers were balled into fists. Time was running out. Agent Jones had repeatedly said time was critical. Sam could see his window of opportunity slipping away...

Then he saw a third person - a man - approaching Rebecca.

Time slowed. Each of the man's steps was slow and heavy - and the raindrops seemed to fall in slow motion. Sam knew this was his moment. The moment to rescue his sister.

He ran for her.

"Rebecca!"

His sister didn't hear him. Sam ran with every ounce of strength. He saw Rebecca's bodyguard turn towards him and was surprised to see that it was a middle-aged woman! Her mouth an 'O' of surprise.

WHAM! Sam tackled Rebecca around the waist and pulled her from the woman's clutches! They both toppled backwards onto the wet deck.

He heard a scream and felt every muscle in his body tense. He was prepared to fight in order for them to escape.

"Rebecca! Run!" he yelled as the woman reached for him. He turned to push his sister away - but then froze...

It wasn't Rebecca. Sam didn't recognise the face of the girl—

SLAP! The girl struck his cheek so hard Sam fell onto his back. He was suddenly aware of a string of angry German coming from the girl, her mother and her approaching father.

"S-sorry!" he stuttered. "I thought you were my sister!"

The woman helped her daughter stand, glaring at Sam as she issued a chain of, what Sam could only assume were, insults.

Sam looked around in confusion - then he saw Agent Jones standing at the other corner of the deck. He was running towards another three figures standing at the barrier.

Sam instantly recognised his sister. She looked pale and frightened. The other was a woman dressed in a long black trench coat and boots. A black headscarf concealing her face, and making her resemble some kind of swashbuckling assassin from a comic book. The third figure was an older man who took a case from the woman and handed over a small watch-sized box.

Jones cannoned into the man too late - the exchange had been made. Sam assumed the older man must be the scientist who was trading the Neural Chip.

Everything happened quickly. The man fell - the case he was handed smashed on the ground and thousands of Euro notes fluttered out. Caught on the wind they blew across the deck in a thick cloud. Surrounding tourists ignored the fight and instinctively went for the fluttering cash. It was instant chaos!

Agent Jones then turned on the woman. She drew what looked like a sword hilt from her long coat and raised it above her head as a wicked black blade extended out!

Jones leapt aside as the blade clanged against a telescope bolted to the deck. The black metal must have been razor sharp as it severed the telescope from its stand!

Jones swung a punch at the woman - but she cartwheeled away in a smooth ninja-like move. Then, in a seamless movement, she brought the sword around again. It was a killing blow - or would have been if Jones hadn't parried it with the broken telescope. With each deflected strike, sparks flew from the sword.

Despite his greater physical strength, Jones was losing out against the ninja's superior fighting skills. She forced him into the corner - then feigned another blow with the sword–

The ninja suddenly stopped the blade mid-swipe and, with a shapely leg, kicked Jones in the face! Jones reeled towards the barrier - propelled by another kick from the woman.

Sam clambered to his feet, ignoring the crying from the girl next to him. He had to help Agent Jones, but how?

He started to run - but felt a hand grab his collar. It was the irate German mother. She pulled him backward, but Sam's gaze was fixed on Jones. Using all of his bodyweight he broke free from the woman's grip. He took several steps... then stopped as the ninja performed a spin-kick with enough force to lift Jones over the safety barrier's edge!

Sam watched in horror as Jones sailed off the edge off the tower! He ran forwards again, feeling

Despite his greater physical strength, Jones was losing out against the ninja's superior fighting skills.

helpless.

"Jones!"

Nobody else was paying attention - they were still scrambling for the cash that fluttered across the platform.

The ninja heard Sam's cry and turned. Her headscarf had pulled away during the struggle - and Sam was shocked to see it was Gail Torrez, the girl who had checked him in at the competition!

She spun to face him. Her eyes widened in surprised when she saw Sam. He caught up with her before she could compose herself. Sam threw a punch that she easily deflected with a martial arts parry.

"You killed him!"

"And you're next!" she purred.

She kicked for him - but her aim was wide as Sam ducked aside.

"HA! Missed!" taunted Sam.

But she wasn't aiming for his head. She had kicked a telescope bolted to the rail. The metal scope spun around on its mount and clobbered Sam across the back of the head! He collapsed to his knees as bright stars filled his vision and a painful jolt ran through his skull.

Sam went for Rebecca's hand. Their fingers touched...

He saw Rebecca's confused expression as she finally recognised her saviour. "Sam? What are–?"

She didn't have chance to finish her sentence before she was yanked backward - her fingers slipping from Sam's grasp.

"'Becca!" he shouted and tried to follow, but the deck seemed to sway under his feet and his vision was blurring from the impact.

He just caught sight of Torrez pulling Rebecca with her as she elbowed her way through the money-grabbing tourists - then lost sight of her as they entered the elevator and the doors swished closed.

Sam tried to stand, but was forced to grip the safety barrier until his head stopped spinning.

The old scientist man was still on the floor where Jones had tackled him, trying to save what money he could. Sam grabbed him by the lapels.

"What did you give her?"

"The chip! She bought my Neural Chip! This is my money! Help me!"

With disgust, Sam shook the old scientist. This man's greed could kill his sister.

"How can I stop it?" Sam demanded. The man was more interested in his money. Sam shook him again. "How?"

The man gasped. He pulled a small card from his pocket.

"Here! The chip's code! Have it! Now help me get my money!"

Sam pushed the man to the floor and examined the card:

KRANNEZA YKZA BWPDKI

He wasn't sure what the language was: Polish or Russian maybe?

Sam pushed his way to the barrier and peered over the edge - fearing what he might see, but also secretly hoping Jones was clinging to the edge.

To his surprise he saw nothing. There was no sign of Agent Jones' crumpled body on the ground below, nor was he hanging by his fingernails.

Sam still felt groggy from the blow to his head. He sucked in a deep breath and pushed his way through the clamouring crowd.

"Move!"

Sam knew he had to get down and follow Torrez, but without Agent Jones to guide him he hesitated.

"Come on, Sam," he said to himself, gathering the courage to go after his sister alone. She was depending on him and he had no other choice.

There was another elevator he could use, but it was in the Tower's opposite leg and from where he was he couldn't see if it was on his deck or not. Then he noticed a sign pointing to the staircase that ran down the centre of one huge leg of the tower.

Sam pelted down the stairs, which were exposed to the elements. The steps were wet and slick. His feet clattered on the metal and several times he was forced to hold the handrail to keep his balance as the flights zigzagged down. He was glad he was descending, as climbing up the 347 steps would have killed him. Luckily everybody else had sense enough not to use the wet staircase so there was nobody to slow him down.

Sam exited from the tower's leg at a run. His legs were numb and shaking, but he refused to give up. He scanned the plaza for his sister. It was surprisingly easy for him to tune out the people milling around and focus only on people who were walking away from him. It was just like selecting the correct enemy from a crowd of civilians in any of his computer games...

Good old *Polybius*, he thought. It must have sharpened his senses.

He spotted Torrez and Rebecca hurrying across the *Champ de Mars*, which was a long park leading away from the Tower. Sam sprinted after them.

Torrez reached a black Land Rover with tinted windows and bundled Rebecca inside.

Sam yelled out, "Rebecca!"

Torrez spun around and was surprised to see Sam a hundred metres away. She reached for the inside of her coat - and Sam froze as she pulled out a pistol. With nowhere else to go - he threw himself on the damp grass as shots rang out. He rolled, knowing that a stationary target was a dead one. The shots sounded awfully close...

THUMP! Something painfully hammered into his thigh. For a moment he was terrified to think that he had been shot. His hand scrambled for his leg, but he couldn't find a wound—

The gunfire suddenly stopped. He peeked up. Torrez climbed into the car and pulled away with a squeal of rubber.

Sam hammered the grass in frustration. He had not only lost his sister's trail, but he was alone without Agent Jones to guide him.

CHAPTER EIGHT

TRACKING THE ENEMY

Slumped in the furthest corner of a fast-food restaurant, Sam lifted a coffee to his lips with shaking hands. He mentally recalled his last movements.

He had returned to the Eiffel Tower to see if he could find out what had happened to Agent Jones, but had continued walking when a dozen police cars arrived at the scene and officers spread out, checking the Champs du Mars and the Tower itself. Sam was certain the gunshots would have been reported and it was only a matter of time before they found security photographs from the observation deck showing him fighting.

Walking as fast as he dared without raising suspicion, he headed for the river and took the first bridge across. Once on the other side he dropped his cap, fake glasses and fatting body warmer into a waste bin. After thirty minutes of aimless wandering he finally spotted a familiar burger logo and headed inside. He ordered food through a combination of the little French he remembered from school and plenty of pointing.

Now warm, almost dry and no longer hungry, he replayed the events through his mind. Try as he might, he couldn't block the horrific image of Agent Jones falling from the Tower - nor the look on his sister's face, a mixture of surprise and confusion when she recognised her brother. Why hadn't she run away from Torrez when she had the chance?

The hot coffee burnt the roof of his mouth. His parents had tried to ban him from drinking any caffeine - they didn't want him any more hyperactive than he already was, but he usually sneaked a cup here and there.

Well, Sam - you're in this on your own. What're you going to do about it?

The most obvious thing to do was to call his parents, who were no doubt enjoying themselves in the hotel. Oblivious to their children's plight, he imagined the conversation if he called them:

Hi Mum. Listen, Rebecca has been kidnapped by an evil enemy Double Agent because we were playing a computer game. But don't worry, we're in Paris and I'm a secret agent now...

That was one option he could immediately ignore.

Jones is dead... that thought sent a chill through his spine. He hadn't had a chance to get to know his mentor very well, but he had never seen anyone killed before. It was terrible; a nightmare he was sure he would repeat in his mind's eye every time he tried to sleep.

Tell the police...

With his limited French, Sam suspected that would be a problem. Besides, could he trust them? He had thought Torrez was on their side but she was the Double Agent. A traitor. Mistakenly kidnapping Rebecca under the belief that she was a top Polybius Agent. Although she didn't know Sam was actually the high scorer, she must have started to have doubts when she recognised him.

The clock was ticking. Torrez now had the

Neural Chip so there was nothing stopping her diabolical experiments. She was out there - somewhere in Paris...

What to do... lost in Paris...

Sam recalled what Agent Jones had told him - if they were separated he should return to the hotel, but what could they do? Time was against him. He suddenly remembered the phone Agent Jones had given him. He fished it from his pocket and was alarmed to see a dent in the rear case. His heart skipped a beat when he saw a bullet was lodged in there! He remembered the feeling of being shot - Torrez hadn't missed him at all! The phone had caught the bullet and saved his life!

He plucked the bullet out of the case using a wooden stirrer from his coffee. It clattered to the tabletop and he examined it. The bullet had been flattened into a disk from the impact. He had no doubt it would have killed him.

Examining the phone revealed that it wasn't a cheap plastic case as he had first thought. It was made out of a tough plastic material and was evidentially bulletproof, well, almost bulletproof.

It dawned on Sam that the old design was intentional to divert unwelcome attention from thieves. If it was bulletproof, what else could it do?

He found the power button and thumbed it on. The screen flashed to life in full colour. In a swirl of ones-and-zeroes, the Polybius eye appeared onscreen. It blinked - then a laser shot from the phone, straight into Sam's eye. He flinched as his vision turned red. It was over in seconds.

"Retina identity confirmed. Rayner, Sam," came a voice from the phone.

"Who are you?" Sam asked, rubbing his eye.

The phone refused to reply. Instead, the eye appeared to blink then a video of Agent Jones appeared.

"If you're watching this then something has happened to me. We're separated or I have been killed."

Sam looked around to make sure nobody was eavesdropping.

"That means you're on your own. But fear not, SQA doesn't abandon its agents. This phone has everything you need to decode ciphers, access our spy satellite network... and it's got a few extra surprises too..."

For five minutes, Sam was swept away as he watched the condensed instructional video on how to use the phone. How it could be used to scan in the Spy Quest logo to access secret files, CCTV, hidden cameras and a whole host of other hi-tech pieces of software that every spy needed.

By the end of it he had worked out that the video was a generic introduction and not aimed at Sam specifically. That meant the information and techniques could be used by anybody on any mission. It still meant that he was still on his own, but at least he now felt he had a virtual sidekick with him.

Sam finished his coffee. Now it was time to act. He recalled the code they had found on Boris. Montmartre - that was the meeting point after the Eiffel tower. He reasoned that Torrez would be heading there. She had almost an hour's lead, but Sam hoped he could still make it in time.

He used the phone's GPS map to locate his position in relation to Montmartre. It was quite a walk and he was just starting to get dry. He found the phone's interface was very intuitive and soon had the Metro map overlaid and could quickly see what underground train he needed to take. He still had his Metro ticket and the nearest station was just around the corner.

Without a real plan, Sam headed out of the restaurant, determined to save his sister.

Observation. That was the key skill any secret agent needs to possess.

Sam ran through the checklist in his head. If he were to write the list of key skills he thought a spy should have it would read: combat ability, camouflage skills, extreme fitness, super gadgets... but during his very short time at SQA, his illusions had been shattered. Observation was the one skill that would keep him alive.

That, and a bulletproof phone.

The Metro trip across Paris was straightforward and uneventful. Yesterday, if Sam had been asked to travel across a foreign city on his own then he would have baulked at the idea. But events in the last twenty-four hours had changed him, forced him to grow up. He now felt more able, more confident - even if he couldn't get rid of the perpetual fear he felt inside.

Sam had found the Polybius game on the mobile phone and had played it during the underground journey to calm his nerves. Agent Jones' instructional video had reminded him that the game was specially developed to work at a *subconscious* level. It was helping rewire his brain every time he played it and he could only hope it was, in some weird way, recharging his spy skills.

It was certainly opening his eyes to the secret messages buried within the game - each time he took a tunnel he now understood that he was solving a cipher. The letters etched on the virtual tunnel walls were covered in a code that he hadn't yet cracked, but his subconscious mind seemed to be doing it for him. At the very least, he felt calm as he arrived at his Metro stop.

Sam exited Anvers station and, after consulting the phone's GPS map, headed up a steep street towards the *Basilique du Sacré-Cœur*. Sam kept his eyes on the map as he strolled down the picturesque streets. His legs hadn't forgiven him after his descent down the Eiffel Tower and walking uphill caused aches in a whole new group of muscles.

Sam finally looked up when the map announced he had arrived at his destination. A hill stretched up to a magnificent white church at the top, capped with large white domes sculpted from travertine stone. A pair of footpaths curved away from each other, winding up the green tree-lined hill in what would be a pleasant walk, if his legs were not jelly.

Next to him was a fairground carousel, which whirled around with a few younger children giggling as they clung to the brightly painted fibreglass horses. Beyond that a small funicular train carried passengers up the steep incline to reach the church.

Sam looked around. His sister should be here somewhere.

He moved away from is exposed position and stood near the carousel, hoping he would blend in with the other children there. Across the road from his position were several brasseries, packed with people sheltering from the rain. They were drinking strong espresso coffee and eating delicious pastries.

Observation...

He scanned the faces in the café but couldn't see Torrez or Rebecca. Perhaps they were at the top of the hill? Surely there must be some clue to help him?

Then he saw it. He laughed to himself - observation really was the key! The black Land Rover Torrez had escaped in was parked on a corner. He regretted that he hadn't memorised the licence plate, but was pretty sure it was the same vehicle.

Rather than walk directly towards it, Sam took a circular route around to avoid drawing attention to himself. He edged closer to the car, unable to see through the tinted side windows if there was anybody inside. He positioned himself so he had a clear view through the windscreen, the only window that wasn't tinted, and noticed that the vehicle was unoccupied.

He slowly approached and tried the door. To his surprise it opened! Inside there was a GPS attached to the window and very little else. He had to admit, Torrez was a tidy kidnapper. Old Sam would have dismissed the abandoned Land Rover immediately, but his new training was making him think things through. He just had to draw the evidence together...

The vehicle had been left in a hurry. Torrez

hadn't even been bothered to lock the doors - which meant she was in a hurry and didn't intend to return to the vehicle. Sam reasoned that she would be in a rush to execute her plan now she knew the SQA were on her trail. The keys were still in the ignition, confirming his theory that she was in a rush.

The use of the car's GPS indicated that she didn't know the area very well. Sam touched the bonnet - it was warm and making PLINKING noises as the rain cooled it. That meant she had only just arrived and must have wasted her hour lead getting here!

Sam was amazed with how his simple observation skills were effortlessly rattling through his head, forming conclusions he would have never otherwise come to.

"Sam, you genius!" he congratulated himself.

The problem was that was all he could tell from the vehicle. They could be *anywhere*. Sam fought against an unconstructive sinking feeling.

You're a secret agent, he berated himself, time to start acting like one!

Then he remembered the instructional video

on his multi-purpose mobile phone. He took it out and flicked through several options until he found the camera. He activated it and aimed the lens at the car.

The camera showed the vehicle in remarkably sharp resolution. Sam selected an option and the image suddenly became a mass of blues, reds, yellows and orange. Heat signatures. The phone's thermal imaging camera displayed the engine as a mass of bright red colours as heat radiated from it. The surrounding wet ground was blue - aside from a pair of very faint greeny-blue footsteps leading from the vehicle and heading towards the winding path leading up the hill.

Sam checked his own footprints, which were indistinguishable from the ground. He deducted that the only reason he could see these faint footprints was because they had been warmed by the heater inside the car, and had only been made in the last few minutes!

It was all the evidence he needed - Torrez was taking his sister to the top of the hill.

Sam hesitated. If he followed along the path there were too many routes hidden by trees and bushes where the Double Agent could ambush him. Sam needed the element of surprise if he was to stand any chance. He quickly walked towards the funicular, deliberately not running so as not to draw attention to himself.

Luck was with him. As he arrived at the funicular the train was about to depart on its short journey upward, pulled up the slope on heavy steel cables. He purchased a ticket and boarded the tiny cable car sized train; crossing his fingers that he would beat his opponent to the top...

The rain had increased by the time Sam exited the funicular. A crowd of multinational tourists had shoved into the car seconds before it had departed, and now Sam stayed with them at the top; they made a handy human shield should anybody be looking for him.

Close up, the pure white stone of the *Basilique du Sacré-Cœur* was even more impressive. Wide steps led up the remaining hillside to a spacious plaza outside the church. It was filled with people, most of whom where carrying umbrellas. Others hung around an observation platform at the bottom of the steps, which overlooked the steep park beyond and the carousel at the bottom of the hill.

Sam carefully scanned the area for anybody who wasn't behaving touristy and admiring the church or the limited cloud-smothered view across the city. Numerous umbrellas blocked most of his view, but on the other hand, they provided him with a little more cover from prying eyes.

He ascended the steps outside the church. The slight elevation afforded Sam a better view. After a minute of searching, he started to feel doubtful. Had he misread the clues? Had Rebecca been dragged here an hour earlier?

Then he saw movement on the edge of the path below him. Torrez appeared, soaked from her hike up the hill. Sam couldn't believe that he had beaten her on the slow funicular train!

She had her arm around Rebecca in a way that looked casual. Obviously it was to prevent his sister from fleeing. She was also one of the few people not carrying an umbrella. Torrez headed straight for an observation telescope mounted on the wall and caught her breath.

Sam rubbed the tender lump on the back of his head where Torrez had struck him with the telescope.

He longed to whack her over the head in revenge. Sam remained hidden by the hordes of tourists as he observed his targets. He wished Rebecca would run, but *something* was keeping her close to Torrez's side.

Torrez was no longer holding Rebecca, but still his sister made no attempt to flee. The Double Agent was waiting for somebody. Torrez quietly spoke to Rebecca. From the look on her face, it wasn't about anything particularly funny.

If Sam tried to approach them directly he would be instantly spotted. He needed a disguise. He eyed a street vendor near the church selling five-euro umbrellas from a battered sports bag. Sam shoved a ten-euro note in the merchant's hand and took the umbrella without waiting for change. He put it up, making sure it was angled towards Torrez. He casually walked towards the wall where she was waiting. He pulled out the mobile phone and accessed a menu option he had seen earlier.

He had a plan - it was desperate, but it might just work.

He pretended to admire the view, making sure the umbrella hid his face and made no move to get any closer to his sister. After several seconds he reasoned that he mustn't appear to be a threat since Torrez was ignoring him. He slowly walked around his sister, so that he was closer to Torrez. Again he made no sudden or suspicious moves and pretended to be disappointed with the cloudy view, even lifting his mobile phone to take a picture - but instead of activating the camera he thumbed an option labelled: 'TASER'.

A pair of small prongs, just five millimetres long, snapped out from the bottom of the phone. Sam spun around and thrust them into Torrez's back. They were too blunt to cause any harm, but they didn't have to be. As soon as Sam tapped a key on the phone several thousand volts charged through the electrodes. Torrez jerked as the electric shock surged through her and she dropped to the floor.

Sam threw the umbrella down and grinned at Rebecca.

"Sam?" She looked around in confusion. "How did you...? What...?"

Sam glanced at Torrez. From the instructional video, he knew the stun gun didn't have enough charge to hurt her, only temporarily paralyse her. Already her fingers were trying to clench. Sam took Rebecca's hand and pulled her towards the funicular. He winked at her.

"Hey nerdinator, surprised to see me? We need to get out of here! I'll answer all your questions later!"

"No! Sam! Wait—" spluttered Rebecca.

Sam spun around - and suddenly bumped into a huge figure lurking behind him. Sam reeled backwards, almost tripping over Torrez as he did.

"Going somewhere, little man?"

Sam recognised the thick Eastern European accent - it was Boris! He smiled at Sam; but it wasn't a pleasant smile. Revenge burned in the giant's eyes.

"Going somewhere, little man?"
Revenge burned in the giant's eyes.

CHAPTER NINE

CAPTIVE

Sam opened his mouth to shout. All he had to do was alert the hundreds of people around them and there was no way the villains could do them harm in public.

Then he felt something hard prod into his back, and Torrez's voice was close to his ear.

"Make any sudden moves and I'll shoot you. Not electrocute you, but shoot you with a bullet. Make a noise and I'll shoot you. If you don't do exactly what I say—"

"You'll shoot me?"

"You learn fast. Where is Jones?"

Sam shrugged. "Last time I saw him you kicked him off the top of the Eiffel Tower."

Boris grunted. "That should've been Boris's job." He rubbed a scar on his head from where Sam had booted the car door into him.

"What do you know of *Project Lycortas?*" Torrez hissed.

Sam hesitated. It was the first time he'd heard the name, but he knew it must be important.

"Everything," he said with an air of confidence he didn't really feel. He took a deep breath and slowly turned to face Torrez. She held the gun neatly in the pocket of her jacket so that, from a distance, nobody could tell she was armed. He was betting that she wouldn't shoot him now, at least not for such a small infraction of her rules. "Do you really think Agent Jones would have sent me in alone? Unprotected?"

He saw the doubt in Torrez's eyes. She quickly scanned the crowds.

"Now would be the perfect time to surrender," he said with a cocky smile.

He stepped closer to Rebecca. This was going to work! She lowered the gun and looked around uncertainly. Then she studied Sam, her eyes narrowing.

"You know, if the SQA were going to shoot me, they would have done it already. They don't tolerate Double Agents." Sam's smile vanished. "Besides, if they did shoot, they might risk hitting your sister." She pulled Rebecca's coat partially open. There was a small lump of plasticine attached to her belt. A wire ran from it. "Plastique explosives, courtesy of our friend Boris here."

Sam looked at his sister with wide eyes. "That's why you didn't run?"

Torrez smiled unpleasantly. "It stopped her giving us a hard time. Mr Boris here is the explosives expert, that's who I was waiting for. I wouldn't dare remove it myself. A stray bullet would trigger it and we'll *all* blow up." She looked around and seemed satisfied. "Not that I think you have any backup at all."

Sam knew the fear he felt inside was showing on his face. He had never been a great liar.

Torrez casually nudged the gun towards the church. "Let's walk." Keeping the children in front, she marshalled them towards the church. Boris kept several metres behind, his eyes scanning the crowd for potential trouble.

They veered off the beaten tourist track and walked around the edge of the church. Ahead, railings prevented visitors from access to the side of the building, but two bars had been bent apart. The area beyond was thick with weeds and tall grass. They passed through, Boris struggling - his huge frame barely squeezing through. Once in the grounds they stopped at a small wooden door that looked frail and rotting. Boris checked it was locked, and then pressed his hand on a concrete post next to the door. Sam was surprised when the top of the post suddenly glowed - it was a hand scanner in disguise.

With a heavy CLUNK the wooden door swung open, revealing the fact that the frail wood was just camouflage for a metal door that would be more at home in a bank vault.

Boris led them down a narrow winding flight of stone steps. Sam guessed they were in the church vaults, possibly even a hidden level beneath that. Naked light bulbs hung from cords overhead, illuminating the way. Their echoing footsteps were the only sounds he could hear.

They reached another door. This one had a hand scanner clearly visible. Boris glanced at Torrez, even he didn't have clearance to enter this new room. Torrez pressed her hand against the pad, and a light rippled across the surface. The door slid back with a hiss and Boris shoved Sam and Rebecca inside.

The huge room was filled with giant monitors, some showing views outside, others were feeds from security camera's and real time satellite images of the earth. Sam noticed one showed the inside of the competition hall in Glendevon, taken from a hidden camera in the ceiling. Computer terminals lay everywhere and numerous thick power cables snaked across the floor.

In the centre of the room was what looked like a dentist's chair. Sam had a feeling of dread the moment he saw it. On closer inspection he realised that dentist's chairs didn't usually have arm restraints. At least not in any of the dentists he'd visited. The flickering illumination from the multiple screens cast moving shadows across the chair, making it look all the more sinister.

"Welcome to Project Lycortas," said Torrez gesturing around. "We are about to make history in the very heart of a major city and nobody is any the wiser. These vaults have never been used for years - even the SQA has no idea they're here."

Torrez handcuffed Sam's hands in front of him. Boris delicately detached the explosive from Rebecca's waist. He carefully removed the detonator then rolled the now-harmless plastique explosive into a ball and stuffed it into his pocket.

Torrez headed for the nearest computer terminal. "If you lied about having backup outside, then I think you also lied about your knowledge of Lycortas."

Sam said nothing. He felt Rebecca's fingers dig into his arm.

"This is some rescue," she hissed at him. "Did you actually have a plan to get us out?"

Sam felt angry. Nothing was going to plan. "I don't care what you think," he directed his anger at Torrez. "You're a traitor!"

"*Traitor? Moi?*" she said innocently, then rolled back her head and laughed. "I bet you don't even know *who* I'm working for? No, you don't do you? The SQA is like that with its young agents. Tell them as little as possible."

"You're part of Oblivion," said Sam. He was satisfied to see the mocking smile disappear from her lips. "Just another rogue spy trying to rule the world. That's really quite sad."

Torrez scowled and tapped commands on the main computer terminal. A large screen suddenly changed to a three-dimensional computer image. The word LYCORTAS burned in the centre. Pulses of light raced across the logo in a hypnotic manner. Sam tore his eyes away, well aware of the possible subliminal effects. He nudged Rebecca hard in the arm to distract her too.

"You're just ripping Polybius off," Sam pointed out.

Torrez snorted derisively. "We're not pirating it as some second-rate piece of software! We're reconstructing it with a greater potential. If schools bothered to teach the classics then you would know Lycortas was Polybius' father." She looked expectantly at Sam and Rebecca. They both shrugged. She sighed. "Gosh... and you're the best agents the SQA has?"

"I wasn't expecting a history lesson," Sam snarled defensively.

"Never mind the history. The point is the SQA's Polybius project is old. It started back in the eighties as

an arcade machine. In fact, your handler, Agent Jones...
he was the very first recruit."

Sam's eyes widened. Torrez smiled knowingly.

"He didn't tell you, did he? Typical. Yes, he
was the first. The machines were rolled out across the
country and unwitting players pushed up the high
scores. But Jones was by far the best. His talents alerted
the SQA's monitoring stations and within minutes he
had been abducted and indoctrinated in the program."

"Abducted?"

"Oh yes. Back then the SQA was very heavy-
handed. Things have changed... a little. While you
may think the SQA are the good guys, I beg to differ.
Since then, Polybius hasn't changed very much. The
gameplay is addictive, involving solving problems as
you combat your enemy. It forces you to work out
the secret codes embedded in the game. The very best
players are the ones who decipher the codes without
even thinking about it. People like you."

She pointed at Sam - then her finger wavered
and moved to Rebecca. "Or you. You see, you have
put me in quite a quandary. We assumed she was the
star Polybius player, that's why I took her. But then I

have to wonder why Agent Jones would bring along her twin brother to save her... unless it meant I had the wrong child."

"I have no idea what you're talking about," said Sam. He hoped playing dumb would keep Torrez on edge.

"Why do you need either of us?" said Rebecca.

"Ah, a smart question for once." She gestured to the screen. "Lycortas is not just an improvement over the Polybius game - it's in a league of its own. I worked at the Agency for many years, and debated how I could use this technology for more creative purposes. That's why I turned my back on them and joined Oblivion. The money and job prospects were much better, and you get more holidays."

She smiled as she paced the room. "You see, Polybius helps you learn and understand code breaking without conscious thought. It makes you learn with each successive play. My idea is the next step. Lycortas reprograms your brain using suggestion and subliminal messages - all hidden away behind an addictive game. It reprograms the player instantly!"

"Reprograms it to do what?" asked Sam. He was

alarmed by the crazy gleam in her eye.

Torrez stopped pacing and crossed her arms. "Anything I ask. Imagine a world, where every child who plays video games on their computer, console, handheld, phone... whatever, is programmed to act on my every command. All I have to do is whisper an instruction and I will have a global army of millions to do my bidding. Not only that, they will already be programmed to be the very best fighters. Laying down their lives without question if I tell them to do so."

"That's crazy!" exclaimed Rebecca.

"It's genius!" Torrez retorted. "All I had to do was buy the Neural Chip from its creator. That grubby corrupt scientist would only sell if I could prove I had the ideal candidate for the experiment."

She glanced at Rebecca. "That's why I had to take you to the trade. He had to be convinced you had the right mind. You see, that was my last problem. Only certain minds are susceptible to Polybius, which is why the Spy Quest Agency can pick agents from the very best. I need Lycortas to work on *everybody*. So my solution is to copy the brain of the very best Polybius agents and feed that information into Lycortas. My program will instantly map that information onto the mind of the dullest person and make them just as susceptible as the very best Polybius mind, turning them into killers.

"The problem I had was that existing Polybius agents are deep undercover and my security clearance at SQA has always been rather low."

"They don't trust you; what a surprise," quipped Sam.

Torrez scowled as she continued. "Agent Jones was a candidate but he was too old, so I had to wait for this new SQA recruitment drive."

Torrez snapped on a pair of rubber gloves and opened the small box she had bought on the Eiffel Tower. She carefully extracted a computer chip from it. "The Neural Chip." With some reverence she inserted it into exposed circuitry in the arm of the fiendish-looking chair. She closed the panel and turned to face them.

"Now, I need to know which one of you is the real Polybius champion?"

Sam and Rebecca exchanged glances. If Sam was chosen and strapped into the chair then there would be no chance of escape. As much as he hated to land his sister in yet more danger it was the only option he had. He winked at Rebecca.

"My sister's the one. She kept getting the high scores at home. Without her I wouldn't have been selected for the competition. I supposed I was just lucky to be playing a game she hadn't finished."

Torrez frowned suspiciously. "Really?"

Sam forced himself to look as innocent as possible. "It fooled you and Agent Jones, didn't it? That's why he dragged me along on this mission. I just thought it would be a laugh."

Rebecca's eyes narrowed. She realised he was playing some trick and hated being set up. Torrez saw Rebecca's reaction and misread it - she assumed Rebecca was furious at her brother for revealing the truth.

Sam continued his defeated act. "That's why you got her, right? She was the one notching up the top score on Polybius. I mean, you only have to look at my competition scores if you don't believe me. I never won anything. How rubbish is that?"

"Boris, put her in the chair."

Sam had forgotten about Boris and jumped when the thug's great hands lifted Rebecca and carried her over to the chair. She screamed and struggled as he pushed her in place. She managed to get in a good slap across the brute's ear before he restrained both her arms then her feet.

Sam watched helplessly as Torrez placed a metal band around Rebecca's head. Wires coiled from the band and trailed to various computers. A pair of plastic clamps on the band were lowered over Rebecca' eyes. Sam winced in sympathy as Torrez inserted clamps under Rebecca's eyelids, forcing her eyes to stay open.

"Leave her alone!" he shouted.

With Rebecca strapped in place and a gag silencing her screams, Torrez walked back to the computer and started a program.

The chair rose two metres into the air and pivoted around to face seven giant screens which where angled inwards to form a hexagonal cone, with the seventh monitor in the middle.

"What are you doing to her?" shouted Sam.

"Duplicating a map of the neural pathways - think of it as scanning in the layout of her brain, before Lycortas deletes her personality." Torrez hit a key on the computer and the screens pulsed with a kaleidoscope of colours. On the monitor, Sam could see a 3D image of Rebecca's brain appear. Different sections highlighted as colours flashed and patterns pulsed. "You better hope she really is the top Polybius player as you said."

"Why?"

Torrez treated him to a cruel smile. "Because, if not, her head will explode."

CHAPTER TEN
THE LYCORTAS EFFECT

The screens pulsed with spiralling multicoloured points of light. From Sam's point of view he couldn't quite see the full effect, but Rebecca convulsed and whimpered.

"Stop it!" shouted Sam.

"The Neural Chip is now duplicating every connection inside her brain," Torrez narrated. "Then Lycortas will reprogram her so she will respond to everything I say. Unless her brain fries and turns to jelly, of course. This is the first time I've tried this."

A trickle of blood started to drip from Rebecca's right nostril.

"You're killing her!" screamed Sam. He couldn't stand watching any more. He had to do something... but what?

He glanced at the computer screen Torrez had initiated. In the movies the hero would have sabotaged the program, but Sam didn't have the skills and was convinced that randomly hitting keys would make matters worse.

Rebecca squealed, despite the gag in her mouth, as she jerked with pain.

Sam looked back at the screen - and a word caught his eye: OVERRIDE CODE. If only he knew it...

What was the writing on the card he had taken from the corrupt scientist? He recalled the text in his mind's eye:

KRANNEZA YKZA BWPDKI

The solution suddenly occurred to him. It wasn't a foreign language - it was another code!

Sam felt his mind race with a speed he had previously wished he'd possessed when sitting exams. Everything Jones had said replayed through his mind at an impossible quick speed. Something about code breaking --

Look out for vowels and repeated letters...

It was almost as if his own imagination had become a computer screen and the code they had discovered flashed in his mind:

KRANNEZA YKZA

Like a computer display he mentally searched for repeating letters and overlaid the words on the screen:

KRANNEZA YKZA
OVERRIDE CODE

He saw it: two Ns matched the two R in 'override'; K represented the first O and the O in code. Without having to decipher the first two words he knew how the code worked, thanks to the short lesson on his mobile phone. It was a Caesar's code, a simple letter swap technique. All he had to do was work out how far along the letters had been jumbled.

Rebecca's anguished yelps broke his concentration. Both Torrez and Boris were watching their experiment with acute interest and Sam had been temporarily forgotten.

Think, he barked to himself...

He pictured the alphabet in his mind. A is a coded letter E, so the entire alphabet is pushed over five places to the right. So the real letter Z would be... he counted five letters back. Reciting the alphabet backwards while under duress was a difficult task...

V! The real letter Z would be a V, so continuing the alphabet from the beginning - A would be coded as a W...

Then something weird happened; something he was certain was because of his Polybius training. A grid flashed up in is mind's eye, as clear as if he were staring at a TV:

A	B	C	D	E	F	G	H
w	x	y	z	a	b	c	d
I	**J**	**K**	**L**	**M**	**N**	**O**	**P**
e	f	g	h	i	j	k	l
Q	**R**	**S**	**T**	**U**	**V**	**W**	**X**
m	n	o	p	q	r	s	t

Y	Z
u	y

All he had to do was decode the actual override word:

BWPDKI

Torrez glanced at the monitor showing Rebecca's mind map. The image was alive with pulsing colours. A spiking graph monitored her heart rate.

"Something's not right. She's close to having a seizure."

Her eyes fell back on Rebecca, keen not to miss a single gruesome observation.

Sam edged towards the computer terminal. He would only have one shot at what he intended to do. His first task was to get out of the handcuffs. He counted himself lucky that he still remembered some of his magic skills, before he had lost himself in spy novels.

Events had moved so fast that the villains hadn't bothered searching him, other than taking his mobile phone, which now sat on top of a control panel. He reached into his pocket and found the small hairgrip Rebecca had left behind. He used his thumbnail to pull the plastic caps from the end, the slid his finger down the middle so the clip expanded out into a long metal strip.

Making sure nobody was watching, he inserted the grip into the handcuff lock and bent it into a right angle. Quickly taking the bent end out and repeating the action on the other side of the lock he bent the tip of the hairgrip into a small step-shape. He inserted it into the lock and twisted - the handcuffs opened with ease. In seconds he was free, but kept his wrists pressed together so it looked as if he was still cuffed...

Boris glance over at precisely that moment and, not seeing anything amiss, returned her gaze back to Rebecca.

With no more time to lose, Sam darted for the computer and typed in the password he had decoded. He hoped he hadn't made any mistakes...

The words 'LYCORTAS OVERRIDE ACTIVATED' appeared on the screen array and the hypnotic images vanished. With a whine of servomotors the chair holding Rebecca swung back to the ground.

"What the—?" began Torrez as she turned around.

Sam had vanished!

"You little pig!" she screamed. "Where are you? What have you done? You'll never get out of here alive! You think you have stopped me? All you have done is forced your sister to go through that torment all over again!"

She marched to the computer terminal and began typing. As her fingers danced across the keyboard she noticed Sam's mobile phone was missing...

SLAM! Sam popped from his hiding place under the desk and crushed Torrez's hand with the taser electrodes from the mobile phone. She howled in pain - then jerked as he activated the taser once again. For the second time in the last hour, Torrez was paralysed from the shock.

Boris was slow on the uptake. He spun around to see his boss slumped on the floor and Sam shoving something into her hands...

"Nowhere to run, little man," growled Boris menacingly in his thick accent.

Sam ignored him and ran across to his sister. He quickly removed the clamps from her bloodshot eyes and began unfastening her arm restraints.

Boris was puzzled as to why the boy wasn't rushing to flee from him like his victims usually did. The thug cracked his knuckles.

"You hear me, little man?"

Sam finally spun around and held up mobile phone. His finger hovered over a button.

"One step closer and I'll blow this place sky high! I've rewired your plastique explosives."

Boris stopped. He had already witnessed what Sam was capable of and didn't doubt him.

Sam freed his sister and she sat upright, blinking furiously. Tears rolled down her face.

"Don't cry," said Sam.

"I'm not, you idiot! My eyes are stinging!" Sam didn't need to ask if she was alright; she certainly sounded normal.

"We're getting out of here!"

They edged towards the door, circling around Boris. The big man took a step towards them, but Sam tutted and waved the phone in warning.

"You're the expert on what damage those explosives can really do," he warned as he reached the door with Rebecca. Luckily it didn't need a palm scan to open from the inside. The door slid aside and they stepped into the corridor - just as Torrez's paralysis wore off.

"Stop them, you moron! You've got the explosives in your pocket!"

Boris blinked stupidly then pulled the balled explosive from his pocket. Sam smiled guiltily as his trick was revealed.

"I really didn't think that would work," he said. Torrez leapt to her feet - but was suddenly yanked backwards. Boris was about to follow Sam - but stopped when his boss shrieked. He saw the problem and ran over to lift the desk.

"Stop!" shouted Torrez, but it was too late.

Sam had handcuffed her to the desk while she had been paralysed. But not only that, he had wrapped a thick electrical wire around the cuffs and the desk leg. As soon as Boris pushed the desk, the wire became taut - and yanked the precious computer equipment off the desk.

The Lycortas computer smashed to the floor in a shower of sparks!

"What have you done?" screamed Torrez. She ran towards the chair, but was dragged to her backside by the handcuffs. "The chip! Check the chip is still there!"

Boris ran to the chair. His massive hands struggled to lift the small flap that housed the chip. After the fifth attempt he finally wedged a pudgy finger under the cover and opened it. The chip had gone!

Torrez's face burned red. "Kill them!"

But Sam and Rebecca had already vanished.

Rebecca had to shield her eyes as they ran outside. The sky was still grey, but the autumnal light was enough to sting her eyes. Sam held her around the shoulders and urged her through the overgrown thickets towards the gap in the railings. Rebecca was still partially blinded from the flashing images and stumbled over roots and junk. They reached the railings.

"Almost there!" Sam said encouragingly. He glanced back in time to see Boris emerge from the church vaults. Sam had considered spending time to block the door, but had decided escaping into a crowded area would better aid their escape. Sam booted his sister up the backside to push her through the gap.

"OW!"

"They're right behind us!" shouted Sam as he scrambled to follow her.

Boris was quick on his feet and covered the uneven ground to the railings just as Sam's foot disappeared through.

Sam grabbed his sister by the arm and ran towards the thickest parts of the tourist crowds, hoping to get lost in them.

BAM! BAM! Gunshots suddenly rang out and the crowd screamed in panic. Within seconds, Sam and Rebecca were exposed targets as everybody dropped to the floor for cover.

Torrez stood behind Boris, a smoking pistol raised to the sky. Her eyes met Sam's.

"Give me the Neural Chip. You will still die but your sister will live... for now."

Sam pulled the chip out. He glanced over the lower balcony - below was a sharp drop to the park. If he jumped from he would no doubt break something. He held the chip over the edge. Torrez laughed.

"That is solid state silicone. You could drop it, but it's very unlikely to break." With her free hand she CLICK-CLACKED the top of the pistol to ensure there was a bullet in the chamber. "That's a chance I am willing to take."

Sam gulped. This was it. He had nowhere to run. With everybody lying on the ground he also had nowhere to hide. He had succeeded in rescuing his sister only to be shot in cold blood. It was evident that Torrez didn't care who witnessed her brutal act.

Sam licked his dry lips. He wouldn't go out without a fight.

"Have it. You've won."

He held out the chip. Boris took several steps forward, partially blocking Torrez's clear aim at him. Sam suddenly saw his chance.

He dropped the chip on the floor - then stamped on it as hard as he could. The silicone broke under his trainer. Connector pins bent out of shape, some snapping off.

It was destroyed.

Torrez's beautiful face twisted in ugly rage.

"You idiot!"

Luckily Boris was blocking her shot. Then a figure appeared behind Torrez. One of the tourists, who had been pressed against the ground, suddenly jumped to his feet with an acrobatic flip and performed a perfect high-kick - booting the gun from the traitor's hands!

Sam did a double take when he saw their saviour's face—

"Sam! Run!" barked Agent Jones.

Agent Jones

CHAPTER ELEVEN
THE ESCAPE

Sam saw the flash of black as Torrez drew her sword hilt and the carbon fibre blade telescoped out. She rounded on Agent Jones.

Sam was almost overwhelmed with relief at the sight of his mentor alive and well. He desperately wanted to run across and help him as Torrez's sword swished down. Jones leapt aside, rolling down a bank of steps as the blade struck stone.

Now a gun was no longer being waved around, the cowering tourists suddenly found their feet and voices and started to run away.

Boris was almost upon Sam and Rebecca - but a surge of tourists cut across the brute's path. When they had cleared, the slow thinking thug realised his targets had vanished too! He searched around - and spotted them running for the funicular.

Sam had one hand around Rebecca, who was still suffering with her eyes. His other hand was extended, roughly shoving people out of his way.

"Move! Outta the way! *Excusez-moi!*"

The funicular was ahead and people were already cramming inside, driven by panic to flee the madmen outside the church. Sam and Rebecca shoved onboard just as the doors closed. Sam drew in a long breath of relief.

"That was close!"

SMASH! The funicular window disintegrated as a rock struck it. Everybody inside yelled and tried to crouch. Sam saw Boris was standing at the end of the sloping track, weighing something in his hand. Sam paled as he recognised it straight away - the ball of plastic explosive! Boris shoved the pencil-sized detonator into the explosive and lobbed it into the train!

Sam reacted instantly - he caught the explosive and hurled it right back out at the thug! His reactions were perfect - but his aim wasn't–

The plasticine material rebounded from the

window frame and was deflected away from Boris where it landed onto the top of the sloped track!

BOOM! The funicular shuddered as the explosives detonated. The cables securing the train severed and the carriage began sliding down the inclined track!

The explosion threw Boris to the floor, but sensing his prey was escaping, he scrambled to his feet and sprinted after the train. He leapt from the platform as the runaway funicular picked up speed during its sharp descent—

Sam heard the THUD as Boris landed on the roof. That was the least of his problems - the train was picking up speed as it whizzed down the slope, completely out of control! The screech of the wheels on the track was just as loud as the wail of those people trapped inside.

Sam shoved his sister flat on the floor.

"Hold on!" he warned.

He looked up in time to see Boris clamber from the roof and perch in the broken window frame. He sneered at Sam.

"Trapped, little man?"

Then the funicular ran out of track.

The metal safety buffer at the bottom of the slope buckled as the train rammed into it at speed. Everybody inside was flung towards the front of the small carriage. Windows shattered as the walls buckled from the impact. The fact the train was full had helped cushion those inside from any serious injury.

The sudden impact threw Boris from his perch on the window frame. He soared right over Sam's head and smashed through the front window, into the metal buffers beyond.

Sam didn't wait around to see if the thug was OK. He didn't care. As soon as the passengers had levered the funicular doors open, Sam pushed Rebecca out.

"Go! Go!" he urged.

Crowds had already formed around the funicular as people rushed to help those injured inside. Sam and Rebecca nimbly wove their way through the crowds and caught their breath at the carousel.

"Are you OK?" he said, checking his sister for any obvious sign of injury.

She nodded. "Next time you win a free

holiday..." she gasped between breaths, "Count me out!"

A wild roar came from the funicular. Boris was angry! People screamed as the brute shoved his way through. He was hurt from the crash, covered in cuts and bruises that made him look more like a wild monster. If anything, his injuries fuelled his rage.

"He's indestructible!" sighed Sam. "Come on!"

He ran towards the brasseries, without a clear escape plan in mind.

"Where are we going?" gasped Rebecca.

Sam looked around, praying Agent Jones would swoop in to save them - but there was no sign of him. He needed to find somewhere safe —

"The car!" he pointed towards the Land Rover.

They jumped inside the vehicle and hit the door locks. Sam knew from previous experience that locks would not stop Boris for long. Rebecca noticed the keys dangling from the ignition.

"If only we could drive this thing!"

Sam closed his eyes - images flashed through his skull. Jones had said every game had been an instruction book. He recalled how the racing game in the competition was overly complicated at first, but had become easier... the knowledge of how to drive the car formed in his mind. He was convinced he could do it properly, unlike the last time when he'd sandwiched Boris between cars.

He was already in the driving seat. His hand automatically went for the ignition key and turned it on.

"Seatbelt!" he barked.

Rebecca looked at him as if he was crazy. "What are you doing? You'll kill us both!"

Without conscious thought, Sam's hand hit the seat control and he edged forward so his feet touched the pedals. Rebecca grappled with her seatbelt when it was clear her brother wasn't listening. He secured his own belt.

Boris was only metres away as Sam's foot pressed the clutch down and his right hand shoved the gear stick into first.

"Have you ever done this before?" Rebecca cried as she locked the seatbelt in.

"Once... in a game! Hold on!"

He raised the clutch and stamped on the

accelerator. The movement felt natural even though he had never done it in real life. The Land Rover surged forward - the engine revving with a throaty growl.

Boris had been running towards them - but suddenly stopped as the 4x4 headed straight at him! The thug reversed direction, his boots slipping on the wet flagstones as the Land Rover accelerated.

Sam had no intention of running the man over - but he couldn't see properly through the rain-splattered windscreen. No matter what driving expertise he had unconsciously been taught, he didn't know where the wiper controls were. His fingers knocked a stalk next to the steering wheel - and the indicators came on. Sam looked at the unfamiliar controls with a frown.

"Where's—?"

Rebecca screamed, "LOOK OUT!"

Sam looked back up in time to see the carousel fill the windscreen! Fortunately nobody was on it, as everybody had rushed to help people on the funicular. Boris had been heading towards the ride for safety.

Sam's foot smashed the brake. But it was too late...

The Land Rover ploughed into the spinning

carousel at speed. Boris jumped - but the nose of the car struck his backside and propelled him with some force against one of the revolving horses! A plastic hoof clobbered him across the head and knocked him out cold. The vehicle splintered a section of the ride apart before coming to a halt. The engine stalled and fell silent. Then the window wipers snickered across the glass.

Sam and Rebecca exchanged glances.

"Oops," said Sam.

"I think we need to get out of here - quick!"

Sam nodded and they both undid their seat-belts as the people began heading over to help.

"SAM!" Agent Jones came bounding down the hill path at a run. He sported many bruises and cuts from his recent fight.

"Where's Torrez?" asked Sam.

"She got away. But that doesn't matter you stopped Project Lycortas, well done!"

"There are an awful lot of unhappy people looking at us!" Rebecca said.

The crowd's expressions of concern changed to anger when they saw that children had crashed the car. Then they did a puzzling thing - they all stopped advancing.

Sam frowned. "What—?"

BAM! Torrez suddenly landed on the vehicle's bonnet! She looked as roughed up as Jones did, and her face was twisted in fury. She arced her sword hilt and the blade snapped out - piercing the windscreen and missing Sam's neck by inches as the tip embedded into the car seat! She quickly retracted it for another stab.

Agent Jones dived into the vehicle, shoving Sam aside. He skilfully turned the engine over and knocked the car into reverse. The sudden movement sent Torrez flailing from the bonnet. She backflipped and landed on her feet, sword ready. Jones reversed at speed and then twisted the steering wheel. The vehicle skidded a full 180° on the wet paving stones.

"She's still coming!" shouted Sam as he peered through the rear window. Torrez ran towards them with grim determination.

Jones put the car into gear and sped forward - narrowly missing an approaching motorcycle, which swerved out of his path.

Sam watched in amazement as the motorcycle

shot past the 4x4. Torrez moved like a striking cobra. She grabbed the handlebars, pulling the front brake on. At the same moment she pushed the rider off and the motorcycle flipped around on its locked front wheel so it was now facing Sam! Torrez leapt on the bike and revved the engine. It had happened so fast Sam couldn't believe his eyes.

Jones adjusted the rear mirror and saw their pursuer.

"Strap in!" he commanded.

Rebecca scrambled into the rear seat and buckled up. Sam took the front seat and locked his belt across the same time Jones did.

They sped down the steep hill, passing parked cars so closely that wing mirrors were ripped off. They hurtled through a crossroads without slowing - narrowly missing a small hatchback that had slammed on its brakes to avoid colliding.

Torrez was forced to swerve around the hatchback. Her bike fishtailed dangerously - the rear wheel striking the small car before she regained control and continued the pursuit.

Ahead, both Sam and Jones could see a busy

street cutting across their path. It was too late to stop. They shot out of the side road at speed—

BAM! A taxi clipped their rear bumper. From inside it sounded as if a firework had gone off. Jones wrestled with the wheel as the Land Rover spun in a complete circle. Smashed debris from the crumpled cars spilled across the road.

It took all of Agent Jones' skill to control the car. They overshot one carriageway of the road and drove along a wide tree-lined walkway situated between the two lanes. Pedestrians scattered from their path as Jones repeatedly hit the horn.

"MOVE!" he yelled.

A quick glance behind revealed Torrez had successfully navigated the wreckage. She revved the motorbike, rearing into a wheelie as she surged forward.

Sam could only watch as she drew alongside and swung her deadly blade. The carbon fibre sword slit through the metal spar between the windscreen and the door and shattered the side window next to Sam. He ducked as safety glass rained down on him and the blade severed the headrest he had been leaning on seconds before.

Jones jerked the wheel and the heavy 4x4 rammed into the bike. Torrez was almost thrown off. She struggled to control the wobbling vehicle - narrowly avoiding a bench on the walkway. She pulled behind the Land Rover.

Agent Jones yanked the wheel - and the vehicle bounced from the walkway and skidded back onto the road. Sam sat up, shaking hundreds of tiny fragments of safety glass from his hair. When he saw the view ahead his fingers dug into the dashboard in fright.

"Wrong way! Wrong way!" he howled.
They were on the wrong side of the road! Jones weaved the vehicle through oncoming traffic - which flashed headlights and blared horns in warning.

"You're going to get us killed!" yelled Rebecca, grabbing Sam's seat to brace herself.

"That's a distinct possibility," muttered Jones through clenched teeth.

A phone suddenly rang. Rebecca patted down her pockets and retrieved Sam's phone from it. She had been playing Polybius when Torrez had abducted her and had forgotten it was there.

"My phone! If that's mum you better not say where you are!" Sam warned her.

It was a withheld number. She answered.

"Hello?"

Sam glanced over Rebecca's shoulder. Torrez was keeping her distance. It looked like she was talking on her mobile phone...

Sam suddenly knocked the mobile from his sister's hand.

"DON'T!"

He could just hear Torrez's voice on the other end. He looked at his sister - her face was blank as the Lycortas programming took over her brain, triggered by Torrez's insidious commands!

Rebecca suddenly lunged for Agent Jones. She moved with purpose - her hands snagging the seatbelt around his throat. She pulled back with all her bodyweight, choking him!

Sam tried to grab her - but his own seatbelt held him back. Rebecca used her foot to shove Sam away. His flailing hand plunged the cigarette lighter down and his elbow accidentally turned the radio on. The car was filled with fast pumping guitar music.

Jones' face was bright red. He let go of the steering wheel so he could use both hands to pull the seatbelt from his throat.

"Snap out of it!" shouted Sam. He slapped Rebecca across the face - and was rewarded with a kick to the stomach that winded him.

"Need... sharp.... shock..." spluttered Agent Jones.

The Land Rover suddenly rocked as they scraped the side of an approaching delivery van at such speeds they swapped paint and the remaining windows imploded! The close call forced Sam back into his seat, just as he was about to try and release his belt and scramble into the rear seat.

Just then the cigarette lighter popped. Sam snatched it out.

"Sorry!"

He thrust the lighter's cherry-red glowing tip into Rebecca's thigh. Her jeans singed then he heard the sharp sizzle of her skin beneath. Rebecca shrieked and fell back in her seat. The pain had been enough to snap her out of Lycortas' spell and regain her senses.

Jones sucked in a deep breath as the seatbelt

slackened from his throat.

"Hold on!" he wheezed in a tiny voice.

He slammed on the brakes. The Land Rover's front angled down on its suspension as it suddenly stopped. Everyone inside was thrust forward. Luckily Rebecca still had her belt on.

Following too closely behind, and gloating over her plan, Torrez had no time to hit the brakes as the Land Rover stopped. She careened into the back of it at speed.

Sam flinched as the motorbike struck them with a noise like an explosion. Torrez has flung over the handlebars - and crumpled into the windscreen of an approaching car that had stopped to avoid colliding with them.

Other vehicles skidded to a halt, some rear-ending others. One slammed into the side of their Land Rover spinning it sideways and buckling the door next to Sam.

Agent Jones climbed out and motioned for Sam and Rebecca to follow. Sam's neck hurt from whiplash, but he couldn't complain - despite everything he was still alive.

Steam rose from under their bonnet. Angry French drivers clambered from their vehicles, shouting at one another. As far as Sam could tell nobody was seriously injured. He looked at Rebecca with concern. She was rubbing her leg.

"Are you OK?"

She looked confused. "W-what happened?"

Agent Jones reached the car Torrez had landed on. The windscreen was a crumpled mess... but there was no sign of her. Jones looked around with concern.

The Double Agent had vanished.

"I still don't get it," said Sam has he reclined back in the comfortable leather seat of the private Learjet. The engines rumbled quietly as they crossed France.

Agent Jones had taken them to a private airfield just outside of Paris. He had explained that the aircrafts here were used exclusively for the SQA, and Rebecca had whooped with delighted when they were taken aboard a small private jet, the likes of which she had only ever seen movie stars travel in. It was the quickest way they could return to Glendevon before their pampered parents became aware that something was amiss.

"Don't get what?" said Jones with a sigh.

"Torrez gets away and Boris is arrested by the local police. It doesn't feel like we've achieved anything!"

Agent Jones laughed, then winced as his ribs started to sting.

"You're not easily pleased, are you? The traitor may have escaped, but at least she was defeated. With the Neural Chip destroyed and her prototype in tatters, she blew her Double Agent cover for nothing. And now SQA doesn't have a mole. We've done great things. You saw what the Project Lycortas was capable of." He looked at Rebecca when he said that. She was already fast asleep in the sumptuous leather chair, her feet curled underneath her.

"Will she be OK?" said Sam with concern. He was glad she was asleep, as admitting concern about his sister was something he could never live down - even after risking his life to save her.

Jones nodded. "When we get back to Glendevon, Dr Patrick has a team on standby to reverse the brainwashing process. We think we can reverse the Lycortas effect, it hadn't had a chance to fully take control. We should be able to blank her memory of the entire incident too." He looked at Sam and smiled. "Only you will remember that you're an SQA operative. Your secret identity is safe!"

Sam leaned back in his chair and thought about his future life as a spy. At least it wouldn't be dull.

"What happened at the Eiffel Tower? How did you survive?"

Jones smiled. "I would like to tell you it was with some super-gadget. In fact there is a safety net around the Tower's edge to prevent people from falling off. Luckily one caught me. Nothing to do with skill, just dumb luck."

"Is this what it was like for you when you became an agent? You were about my age, weren't you?"

Agent Jones looked at Sam in surprise, then shook his head sadly. "For me it was... worse in some ways. The SQA took me away from my friends and family. I was in the UK because my parents worked in banking and we'd left America behind. Back then the

SQA was a new unit. Nobody knew if Polybius would work. They were unsure how to recruit new agents."

"Didn't you ever want to go back and see your family?"

Agent Jones thought for a long moment. "I did. But what I was doing was cool too. I regret not going back to see them and reassuring them I was OK." He looked sad. "That was a mistake. But not a mistake SQA will repeat. My re-launched Polybius program is much more sophisticated. We won't have to pull you away from your family, for example. Pretty soon we'll have Polybius machines across the country, across the world. Located in schools, libraries, hotels... anywhere we can recruit new agents."

Sam leaned back in his chair. Despite the terrifying near death encounters that he had experienced in the last twenty-four hours, he had had... fun was the wrong word. Adventure was closer to what he was thinking. He knew that his life was about to get a whole lot more interesting.

He glanced out of the window. It was dark outside. The land below was lit up with a network of white and orange lights that formed roads and cities.

He wondered how many more young secret agents were down there, waiting for their opportunity to be recruited...

HOTELS AND RESORTS

Spy Quest is available to play at the following hotels and resorts;

United Kingdom
Glcneagles Hotel, Auchterarder, Perthshire, Scotland

Hilton Grand Vacations at Craigendarroch, Braemar Road, Ballater, Scotland

Macdonald Aviemore Resort, Aviemore, Inverness-shire, Scotland

Macdonald Crutherland House Hotel, Strathaven Road, East Kilbride, Scotland

Center Parcs - Whinfell Forest, Penrith, Cumbria, England

Center Parcs - Sherwood Forest, Nottingham, England

Center Parcs - Elveden Forest, Suffolk, England

Center Parcs - Longleat Forest, Wiltshire, England

Center Parcs - Woburn, Bedfordshire, England

America

Sheraton Vistana Resort, 8800 Vistana Centre Drive, Orlando, Florida 32821

Sheraton Vistana Villages, 12401 International Drive, Orlando, Florida 32821

The Westin Kierland Resort & Villas, 15620 North Clubgate Drive, Scottsdale, Arizona 85254

Westin Ka'anapali Ocean Resort, 6 Kai Ala Drive, Lahaina, Maui, Hawaii 96761

Westin Princeville Ocean Resort, 3838 Wyllie Road, Princeville, Kaua'i, Hawaii 96722

Westin Desert Willow Villas, 75 Willow Ridge, Palm Desert, California 92260

Westin Mission Hills Resort & Spa 71777 Dinah Shore Drive Rancho Mirage, California 92270

Sheraton Desert Oasis, 17700 North Hayden Road, Scottsdale, Arizona 85255

Vistana's Beach Club & PGA Resort, 10740 South Ocean Drive, Jensen Beach, Florida 34957

Sheraton Mountain Vista Villas, Avon / Vail Valley, CO 81620

Westin Riverfront Mountain Villas, Lakeside Terrace Resort, 160 West Beaver Creek Blvd, Avon, CO 81620

Orange Lake Resort, 8505 Irlo Bronson Memorial Highway, Kissimmee, Florida 34747

Wyndham Bonnet Creek Resort (Walt Disney World), 9560 Via Encinas, Lake Buena Vista, Florida 32830

U.S. Virgin Islands
Westin St. John Resort & Villas, 300A Chocolate Hole, St. John, U.S. Virgin Islands 00831

Mexico
Westin Lagunamar Ocean Resort, Blvd Kukulcan KM 12.5 Lote 18, Zona Hotelera, Cancun, Quintana Roo 77500, Mexico

We are always adding resorts to our list, so check out the website for where you can play it and for the latest news about upcoming books!

As a special gift, we are offering a voucher on the next page for every book owner to play a Spy Quest game for themselves. The offer is only available at participating hotels and resorts. To claim your free game, please present the book to the appropriate member of staff within the resort and they will issue you with your exclusive Code Name and Password.

Do you have what it takes to become an SQA Agent ? We'll be watching to see how you get on!

SPY QUEST
CLAIM YOUR FREE GAME*

At participating Hotels and Resorts only

Code Name.........................

Password.........................